Prisons

Other books in the Social Issues Firsthand series:

SOCIAL ISSUES
FIRSTHAND

Prisons

Mary K. Hill, Book Editor

GREENHAVEN PRESS

An imprint of Thomson Gale, a part of The Thomson Corporation

THOMSON

™

GALE

Detroit • New York • San Francisco • New Haven, Conn. • Waterville, Maine • London

Christine Nasso, *Publisher*
Elizabeth Des Chenes, *Managing Editor*

For more information, contact:
Greenhaven Press
27500 Drake Rd.
Farmington Hills, MI 48331-3535
Or you can visit our Internet site at http://www.gale.com

LIBRARY OF CONGRESS CATALOGING-IN-PUBLICATION DATA

Prisons / Mary K. Hill, book editor.
    p. cm. -- (Social issues firsthand)
  Includes bibliographical references and index.
  ISBN-13: 978-0-7377-3605-2 (harcover : alk. paper)
  ISBN-10: 0-7377-3605-4 (hardcover : alk. paper)
  1. Prisons. 2. Prisoners. 3. Prisoners' families. 4. Correctional personnel. I. Hill, Mary K.
  HV8491.P75 2007
  365--dc22
                                                                    2006020091

Printed in the United States of America
10 9 8 7 6 5 4 3 2 1

Contents

Chapter 1: Life in Prison

A man searches for understanding and purpose during his time in prison, exploring his thoughts in a journal he has kept for ten years.

A prison inmate details the horror of being raped by a cell mate in a Texas prison. He writes that rape in prison is a form of torture allowed because of lax prison policies.

A man who is serving two life sentences describes the impact that the suicide of a cell mate had on him.

A former inmate reports on prison conditions for female prisoners in a Canadian prison, writing that the women live in degradation and fear in segregated areas within a men's maximum-security penitentiary.

Chapter 2: Prison Guards, Staff, and Volunteers

An educator describes her work in a county jail as the most rewarding teaching experience of her life.

A rookie correctional officer argues that his job is honorable because he works to keep the public safe and help offenders become law-abiding citizens.

Foreword

Social issues are often viewed in abstract terms. Pressing challenges such as poverty, homelessness, and addiction are viewed as problems to be defined and solved. Politicians, social scientists, and other experts engage in debates about the extent of the problems, their causes, and how best to remedy them. Often overlooked in these discussions is the human dimension of the issue. Behind every policy debate over poverty, homelessness, and substance abuse, for example, are real people struggling to make ends meet, to survive life on the streets, and to overcome addiction to drugs and alcohol. Their stories are ubiquitous and compelling. They are the stories of everyday people—perhaps your own family members or friends—and yet they rarely influence the debates taking place in state capitols, the national Congress, or the courts.

The disparity between the public debate and private experience of social issues is well illustrated by looking at the topic of poverty. Each year the U.S. Census Bureau establishes a poverty threshold. A household with an income below the threshold is defined as poor, while a household with an income above the threshold is considered able to live on a basic subsistence level. For example, in 2003 a family of two was considered poor if its income was less than $12,015; a family of four was defined as poor if its income was less than $18,810. Based on this system, the bureau estimates that 35.9 million Americans (12.5 percent of the population) lived below the poverty line in 2003, including 12.9 million children below the age of eighteen.

Commentators disagree about what these statistics mean. Social activists insist that the huge number of officially poor Americans translates into human suffering. Even many families that have incomes above the threshold, they maintain, are likely to be struggling to get by. Other commentators insist that the statistics exaggerate the problem of poverty in the United States. Compared to people in developing countries, they point out, most so-called poor families have a high quality of life. As stated by journalist Fidelis Iyebote, "Cars are owned by 70 percent of 'poor' households.... Color televisions belong to 97 percent of the 'poor' [and] videocassette recorders belong to nearly 75 percent.... Sixty-four percent have microwave ovens, half own a stereo system, and over a quarter possess an automatic dishwasher."

However, this debate over the poverty threshold and what it means is likely irrelevant to a person living in poverty. Simply put, poor people do not need the government to tell them whether they are poor. They can see it in the stack of bills they cannot pay. They are aware of it when they are forced to choose between paying rent or buying food for their children. They become painfully conscious of it when they lose their homes and are forced to live in their cars or on the streets. Indeed, the written stories of poor people define the meaning of poverty more vividly than a government bureaucracy could ever hope to. Narratives composed by the poor describe losing jobs due to injury or mental illness, depict horrific tales of childhood abuse and spousal violence, recount the loss of friends and family members. They evoke the slipping away of social supports and government assistance, the descent into substance abuse and addiction, the harsh realities of life on the streets. These are the perspectives on poverty that are too often omitted from discussions over the extent of the problem and how to solve it.

Greenhaven Press's Social Issues Firsthand series provides a forum for the often-overlooked human perspectives on society's most divisive topics of debate. Each volume focuses on one social issue and presents a collection of ten to sixteen narratives by those who have had personal involvement with the topic. Extra care has been taken to include a diverse range of perspectives. For example, in the volume on adoption, readers will find the stories of birth parents who have made an adoption plan, adoptive parents, and adoptees themselves. After exposure to these varied points of view, the reader will have a clearer understanding that adoption is an intense, emotional experience full of joyous highs and painful lows for all concerned.

The debate surrounding embryonic stem cell research illustrates the moral and ethical pressure that the public brings to bear on the scientific community. However, while nonexperts often criticize scientists for not considering the potential negative impact of their work, ironically the public's reaction against such discoveries can produce harmful results as well. For example, although the outcry against embryonic stem cell research in the United States has resulted in fewer embryos being destroyed, those with Parkinson's, such as actor Michael J. Fox, have argued that prohibiting the development of new stem cell lines ultimately will prevent a timely cure for the disease that is killing Fox and thousands of others.

Each book in the series contains several features that enhance its usefulness, including an in-depth introduction, an annotated table of contents, bibliographies for further research, a list of organizations to contact, and a thorough index. These elements—combined with the poignant voices of people touched by tragedy and triumph—make the Social Issues Firsthand series a valuable resource for research on today's topics of political discussion.

Introduction

Despite decreases in crime rates in the United States, the nation's prison population has increased by more than 50 percent since 1991. In fact, America has the largest prison population of all industrialized countries. By 2004 one out of every 138 U.S. citizens had been incarcerated or was behind bars. Experts point to two main reasons for the increased imprisonment rates in America. First, many states have adopted three-strikes laws that keep criminals behind bars for life after a third offense. The second reason, some argue, is America's war on drugs, which has led to the incarceration of many drug addicts and dealers.

Critics of the prison system argue that the explosion in the prison population represents a failure in America's crime policies. They contend that prisons fail society because they punish not only criminals, but also the children of prisoners who grow up without a mom or dad active in their lives. Some critics also argue that prisons hurt society because when people are imprisoned for long periods, communities do not get the benefit of their potential contributions and talent. Various proposals have been made to reform the prison system, including a model known as restorative justice.

Restorative justice is based on the principles of accountability and forgiveness. According to the theory of restorative justice, it is wrong to give long prison sentences to people who commit crimes. Instead, advocates argue, wrongdoers should have to meet with the victims of their crimes and work to heal the harm caused by their crime. The criminal is also expected to repay the victim for the offense. Sometimes the repayment can involve a short jail sentence and the payment of money for damages, or service to the victim and the victim's community. Proponents believe that this restorative justice process helps the victim to forgive the perpetrator and let go of the pain of the crime. Restorative justice is practiced mainly in Europe as well as in countries including New Zealand, Australia, and Canada. Some communities are also beginning to adopt its practices in the United States.

Restorative justice is more than just a concept to Russ Kelly, a volunteer for the Community Justice Initiatives of Waterloo Region of Canada. After Kelly was convicted of vandalizing twenty-two properties in one night, he became one of the first criminals prosecuted under the Victim Offender Reconciliation Program, started in 1974 in Elmira, Ontario. Instead of going to prison, Kelly and his codefendant were ordered to meet their victims and apologize for the damage they had done. They also were required to pay $550 restitution and a $200 fine. The men were also placed on eighteen months' probation.

Today Kelly is a strong advocate of the restorative justice model, which he says changed his life. Kelly writes, "I am not proud of what I did; however, I am extremely proud of what has become of it. It still amazes me that something so wrong could result in something so good that has affected many, many lives in a positive way."[1] Kelly and many restorative justice practitioners argue that restorative justice is the answer to high rates of incarceration and criminal recidivism. They cite studies of community programs that show restorative justice practices have reduced the recidivism rates of nonviolent offenders.

Proponents of restorative justice argue that in addition to having a positive impact on offenders, restorative justice practices benefit the victims of crime. Several major studies indicate that up to 80 percent of victims that go through the conference process of meeting with an offender who committed a crime against them are less fearful of being revictimized. One such victim named Helene lives in the Thames Valley in the United Kingdom. Helene became involved in the restorative justice process after criminals repeatedly vandalized and stole her car. Helene reports that going through the restorative justice process was healing for her:

> As soon as the 15-year-old youth looked at me and said how sorry he was for what he had done, I felt a hundred times better than I would have believed possible. He not only apologised for stealing my car, but also for all of the consequences that his choice had led to.
>
> He was absolutely horrified when he was told what had happened to my family. He thought he had stolen a car, but by listening to me he realised he had actually done far more than he ever intended.[2]

She added that she was so impressed with the process that she applied and was accepted for the position of restorative justice administrator with the Thames Valley Police. She concludes, "I feel passionately about Restorative Justice and now I am helping participants to identify and repair the harm and move through the recovery process."[3]

While restorative justice practitioners claim that restorative justice can bring about lasting societal change and curb criminal behavior, some critics argue that restorative justice is not a panacea for crime and the prison population explosion. They believe that not enough research has been conducted on restorative justice practices to understand their long-term impact, especially in the case of those who commit serious, violent crimes.

Critics of restoration justice include feminists and advocates for battered women. Kathy Maller, executive director of Aboriginal Ganooramage Justice Services of Winnipeg, Canada, states that the use of restorative justice in cases where a woman is battered by a spouse or boyfriend raises concerns about safety and protection of the rights of victims. Maller said in a recent article that battered women feel powerless and revictimized when they have to face their abusers in a restorative justice session. She presents as an illustration the case of an Inuit woman who agreed during a restorative sentencing circle to go to couples counseling with her abusive husband only because she was scared of him.

Concerns for the safety of women were also strongly expressed at a national conference held in Canada on the use of restorative justice practices in cases of domestic abuse and violence against women. Irene Smith, the executive director of the Avalon Sexual Assault Centre in Halifax, Nova Scotia, pointed out during the conference that reintegration of the offender into the community, a stated goal of restorative justice advocates, alarms her. "Reintegration of the offender into the community, in our experience, with women who have experienced crimes of sexual assault, creates a great deal of fear and as a matter of fact, re-victimization, not healing, for the survivor."[4] Smith and many activists are concerned that restorative justice practices will also lead to an increase in violence against women. As Smith noted during an interview, her "real concern is that these [restorative justice] initiatives will decriminalize sexual violence."[5]

Concerns that restorative justice practices benefit the offender more than the victim have been raised by many conservatives, including talk show host Bill O'Reilly and Joshua Marquis, the Clatsop County district attorney and vice president of the National District Attorney's Association. O'Reilly and Marquis agreed during a 2006 broadcast of the *O'Reilly Factor* on Fox News that restorative justice is a "new age" approach that coddles criminals. They cited a recent case in Vermont in which a judge who believes in restorative justice principles sentenced a man convicted of repeatedly raping a girl to only sixty days in jail. Marquis also argued that restorative justice practices place the rights of the offender above the rights of victims.

Scholarly critics such as Declan Roche and Kathleen Daly also argue that restorative justice advocates tend to have an overly idealistic view of criminals and victims. Roche argues in the first chapter of his book *Accountability in Restorative Justice* that restorative justice practices ignore the reality of human nature:

> In explaining the dynamics of a [restorative justice] meeting, advocates often draw analogies with the way conflicts are resolved in a loving family, or in a small town. . . . The problem, however, is that the very informality which allows people to show their best side provides the same opportunity for them to show their worst. Just as people can empathize, reconcile, repair, reintegrate, and forgive, so too can they scold and stigmatize, hector and humiliate. . . . There is a great risk in designing a system of justice around idealistic aspirations.[6]

Daly also warns about relying on restorative justice to solve criminal problems. She writes that advocates of restorative justice might be promising too much and that in many cases, the practice is not successful in leading offenders to live upstanding lives, helping victims feel that justice has been served, and repairing social bonds.

Debate will likely continue over whether or not restorative justice can solve the major issue of how society should deal with people who have committed criminal acts. In *Social Issues Firsthand: Prisons*, the authors, including current and former prisoners, the relatives of inmates, and those who work in prisons, provide a variety of personal views about prisons. Given the magnitude of the social issue of prisons in America, having a greater insight into people's experiences with prisons and prisoners is vitally important.

Notes

1. Russ Kelly, "Stories of Reconciliation," Centre for Restorative Justice. www.sfu.ca/crj/index.html.
2. Quoted in Thames Valley Police, "RJ: A Victim's Story," Thames Valley UK Restorative Justice Program. www.thamesvalley.police.uk/news_info/info/rj/victim-story.htm.
3. Quoted in Thames Valley Police, "RJ: A Victim's Story."

4. Quoted in Provincial Association of Transition Houses of Saskatchewan (PATHS), "Restorative Justice: Is It Justice for Battered Women? Report on PATHS' April 2000 Conference." www.hotpeachpages.net/canada/air/rjConference.html.
5. Quoted in PATHS, "Restorative Justice."
6. Declan Roche, *Accountability in Restorative Justice*. Oxford: Oxford University Press, 2003.

Life in Prison

Journal of a Prisoner

David Lightner

In the following excerpts from his prison journal, David Light-ner, winner of the 2005 PEN America Prison Writing Contest in the memoir category, discusses his daily struggles in the Idaho Correctional Institution at Orofino. Lightner describes his life in prison as isolated and sometimes violent. He also writes about his efforts to be allowed the privilege of owning a personal dic-tionary, and the hot miserable days of summer in prison. He ends his winning entry by detailing his dreams for a better world. PEN America Center sponsors an annual writing contest for any prisoners incarcerated in a federal, state, or county prison in the year before the September 1 deadline. The contest also in-cludes categories for poetry, fiction, essays, and drama. PEN's Prison Writing Program also publishes a free handbook for pris-oners, provides one-on-one mentoring to inmates whose writing shows merit or promise, conducts workshops for former inmates, and seeks to publish inmates' work.

October 27, 1998 I began this day much like I begin every day here in prison. I woke at about 6 A.M. to pill call. I always wake up hearing the guard knock on my neighbor's door, and I jump right up and try to get to the door before he knocks on mine. I take my Paxil (20mg, for depression) and I'm up for the day.

I haven't always been one to get right up out of bed—in prison, or at home—but recently I began practicing Hatha Yoga, Meditation, and Pranayama (breath control exercises). The yoga exercises are supposed to be done on an empty stomach. . . .

. . . OK, I got distracted for a moment listening to a con-versation between two guys in nearby cells: One guy asked his buddy, "Do you have a TV?" His buddy answered, "No, but I've got a TV Guide." I thought that was pretty funny.

So, I was doing my first exercise in Hatha Yoga this morning—the corpse pose—and I got a little visualization. I imagined I heard God talk to me and tell me to come to his altar and I saw myself at his altar drinking from a cup . . . and that was that. I didn't think much of it, but as I continued to relax I thought to myself, "Does God really talk to me?" "Yes, God talks to me." "Yes, I talk to you all the time," I heard inside my head. "I have always been talking to you—from the beginning." . . .

Silence and Other Topics

Topics for today's entry: 1) What it means to me to have a dictionary and why it is wrong for a prisoner to be denied a personal dictionary. 2) Silencing the lips for a day—taking a vow of silence and keeping it is not easy. What does it require? How much more difficult is it to quiet the talking in the mind for just five minutes? What does it require to silence the mind? 3) What does it mean to let go? To live in the here and now, with no attachment to the past, the future, life, or material possessions? When this is achieved can anything hurt you? How free from suffering can you become when you have let go and are truly living in the moment? 4) When the mind finally becomes quiet, will God talk?

Silence: Maybe I ought not to have waited until three in the afternoon to write about silence. The tier is much quieter in the morning. Everybody is sleeping. But this isn't what I want to write about. These things are external and I must journey inward; into my thoughts, my feelings most of all; the inner workings of my soul. This is not going to be easy for me, I can see already. But that is why I must do it. I am afraid to write down my deepest feelings. I am also afraid to admit those feelings to myself. Maybe I am afraid to see the monsters that may be revealed when my thoughts are exposed to the light of day—my true and real thoughts unbidden. Yes, I am even afraid to be honest in my own journal lest it be confiscated by the authorities and used against me at some point in the future.

My fear is justified. Big Brother is watching—it's not just my paranoia. They have stolen my writings before—suicide letters to nobody—and then had the balls to sit there and read from them out of my file. I haven't bothered to ask for them back because they are now the property of the state. I wonder—is each page I write just another page added to that file? I am tempted not to write at all—out of self-preservation, or fear, really. But no! I must write! And I must find a way to write truthfully and meaningfully about what matters, regardless of the potential consequences—regardless of my fears. I cannot let myself be oppressed. Not when the stakes are this high.

I'm tired of holding it all in. I'm tired of being silent about the things that matter.

So now I guess I can write a little about silence—silence of speech and silence of environment. Auditory silence. Like I said, I can sometimes get some silence in the morning around here—no radios, no TVs, no yelling—everybody is sleeping. This is when I do my yoga—Salute to the Sun, which I've only been doing for a few days; and my meditation and pranayama. When it is quiet I can do these things more easily, though my concentration is better now than it has been in the past. . . .

Holding On to Life

OK, now I've got this piece of paper in a three-ring binder, which I just purchased from the commissary for $3.03 plus tax. I thought that it might be slightly awkward or uncomfortable writing like this, and it is, but I think I can live with it. I'll try it out for a few days. Maybe if I don't write all the way across the page, but only this far (about 2/3 of the way across the page) it won't be so awkward. In a thousand years it probably won't matter anyhow so I'll just do what comes naturally and keep on writing because I'm going to write from now until the day I die—whether that be near or far. I will write while I live and shall only cease when I die.

Speaking of dying . . . I love life! I don't want to die. Even though I've tried to kill myself so many times, the truth is, I want to live. I love life! . . .

June 22, 2004 It has been five years and eight months since I made that journal entry. I am still in prison. I have not left prison. I have grown and changed in many ways; have had notable successes and failures; but I am still rotting here in prison. I am, right now, in the process of typing out some journal entries I am hoping to publish. I want to fill in some of the blank spots in the journal that I think are important, but I don't want to just go back and add things that didn't exist before, or otherwise compromise the chronological integrity of my journal. So, when I want to do so, I will annotate the journal, but I will record the date on which the new material was actually written. This is kind of a neat idea—like having a conversation with myself and myself-from-a-different-time: literary time travel.

Note 6/22/04: This journal entry was written while I was in solitary confinement, or in prison jargon, Administrative Segregation [AdSeg]. I was, at that time, going to court for felony escape charges, and was in AdSeg due to my being perceived as an escape risk. I ended up getting an additional five years in prison for the escape, and I also ended up doing five years straight in solitary. If I seem a little more bitter it's because I am and that's why. Truth be told, I did get a short break from my solitary confinement in the end of 2001. I was released from AdSeg and sent to the prison up North. That lasted about a month before I wrecked an entire cell in protest of crappy service and was promptly shipped back South. But aside from that short sojourn I spent half a decade without the slightest human contact. If I ever become a mass murderer you can blame it (in part) on that.

As I was typing out my journal entry from October 27, 1998, I realized that I never completed writing about all the topics I intended to write about that day. I want to do that now.

The Importance of a Dictionary

What does it mean to have a dictionary, and why is it wrong for a prisoner to be denied a personal dictionary?

Back in 1998, when I was in solitary confinement, I was not allowed to have a dictionary. The prison would only allow me to have one religious book, but no other personal books. I was allowed to check out two books from the prison library, but they didn't have a decent dictionary.

I spent about three to four months with no way to look up words I did not know how to spell or did not understand. I wanted to do some serious studying and writing, but how serious can my studies be when I am unable to use new words or read and understand material with unfamiliar terms?

I was so frustrated by this injustice that I eventually filed a civil rights lawsuit against the prison claiming violation of my First Amendment rights. The rule eventually changed and I was allowed to have two (2) personal books. I chose to purchase the *New Shorter Oxford English Dictionary* [*NSOED*]. I finally received it in February 1999, and have had it ever since. In fact, as I sit here in my plastic chair, with my typewriter set up on the top of my green metal locker, my trusty *NSOED* sits right here beside me. This dictionary is so important to me that I have hung on to it for over five years. And I know when I walk out the prison gate in 2008 I'll still have it with me. I've possessed and relinquished many material possessions in my life, but there have been very few I have hung on to for as long as I have already hung on to this dictionary. That's how important it is to me. Maybe I don't use it every day, or nearly as often as I could, but having it there when I do need it opens up a world of possibilities that would not exist were I without it.

Now, obviously, I've got a typewriter too. This is a big deal to me. I like being able to write quickly and neatly. I like being able to draft up professional-looking documents, or write letters that command a little more respect than something written out longhand. I've got all the basic tools to do some serious writing; now let's see what I do with them. Yeah, right. I'm already a *real* writer. At least, as much so as I'll ever be, whether or not I publish.

Flashback: October 30, 1998

It is easy to believe that all is lost, and that there is no hope for me, and then to throw it all away—burn all of my bridges. The idea is tempting for some reason, but I must resist the belief, the idea, and the action. OK, well maybe I shall not resist it, but rather I shall let it pass unnoticed, not giving it any power over me.

But should I hope? Hope that all is not lost? Should I cling to some vision of a future for myself? No. I can't do that either. I must let it all go—let it all die. And if it lives of its own accord, then so be it. And if it fades away and disappears—farewell. Farewell. I shall live for today and let tomorrow take care of tomorrow. Because all that I have is today—and Now is Forever anyway. If I can live right now—and just be here now, that is worth a thousand tomorrows. But to do that I need to let go of fear and desire.

These are worthy goals. Let them be my only goals—my only purpose. Live fully in this moment. Let go of hope, fear, desire. Let go of myself, and my future. Experience the Love of Life—the RIGHT-NOW—this very moment.

Easy to say, Grasshopper! Not so easy to do. . . .

Violence on a Cell Block

Last night someone got hurt badly over on C-block. I hear they found him beat down, in his cell. I heard the Code Blue and then, looking out my window I saw the white Dodge prison patrol truck speed out the driveway, his blue and yellow flashers on, and zip up to Pleasant Valley Road. I figured he drove out there to escort in an ambulance. About five minutes later this was confirmed. An ambulance came speeding south on Pleasant Valley and then, with the prison escort leading the way and both lights flashing, the ambulance drove up the main prison road and into the prison. Many of the guys on the unit became excited at the sight of all the colorful flashing lights.

Well, I think I know who the guy was that got hurt. I bet it was D—, the guy I was on C-1 with back in September. I heard that some guy called C—was the one who beat D—up before, so I wouldn't be surprised if it happened again. I'll find out the details later.

What I wanted to write about all this violence is that it scares me. I have had my share of violence and fear in this institution and I think it is wrong. I don't think I should have to be subject to it and I'm going to do what I can to be sure something similar does not happen to me. That was why I escaped and I'm not going to change now. I am committed to avoiding violence—whatever the cost. That cost may be very high because this is a violent part of a violent world and in my desire for non-violence I am probably a minority. I don't like violence and I don't resort to it, except under exceptional circumstances. I certainly will not submit to violence. But there are many twisted people in here who derive a sadistic pleasure from inflicting harm on others. Maybe I will go into protective custody. I have to weigh my options but whatever I choose I will go with it wholeheartedly and I will know that I am right and that God is with me.

Note: Twenty-four hours after writing the above I re-read it and got scared that I had written it down. Typical. But I'm not going to take it back and I'm not going to stop writing. I'm not going to let fear control me. Love and Creativity are Real. Fear and destruction are not. . . .

Still Looking for Answers

August 13, 2003 If I've accomplished anything in the last five years it must be something internal and intangible, as I am still here in this cell, still struggling, still looking for answers.

Or maybe not. On second thought I am certain I have changed both inside and out, and almost completely for the better. They say every cell in our body is replaced about every ten years, so I guess I'm half the man I used to be.

Looking back through my journal from 1998 I see quite a different person. And yet the same. My goodness, my gracious, my God! Why was I cursed with this unrelenting drive to ask the Big Questions? I'm not a philosopher. I feel like I'm a snail blindly sliming my way across a landscape of infinite crab-grass—going nowhere, one blade at a time. Or rather, I should say, I used to feel that way. Now it's a little different. I still feel like a snail tossed upon some suburban joker's lawn, but I understand there's nowhere to go. Nowhere to go. Nothing to change or be changed.

And yet I still go. Back in April, there for a few weeks . . . and in early May, I felt like I had broken through to Samadhi or Nirvana or Enlightenment. I had finally surrendered to my deeper Self—to my little dreamer—and felt as though I could do anything. I'm not going to try to explain it because I did try already and it went away. . . .

But then I think, as hard as my journey has been, it has still been mine. To have the answer without understanding its worth and value, or the meaning of the question (were that even possible) would be quite pointless. The struggle has made the answer mean something. . . .

Yes, I will write. I will write till the day I die. Yes, I will speak, be there ear to hear me or not. But I can see a vision of something greater. The other side is very close. The eternal. The divine. The transcendent. And though there is a wall that keeps me here in the mundane world, that wall also has doors—doors through which I am learning to pass.

My heart tells me to open those doors and let the warmth and laughter of that world spill over into this. My heart tells me that music and image are the language I must use. I can see it all so clearly now. The power is awesome. The ecstasy. The radiance. It is a movie playing in my mind's eye and a soundtrack in my heart. My heart says, "Follow me!"

Who am I to argue with my Heart.

Miserable Days

July 25, 2004 It is a miserably hot and sticky day. This cell is too small for two people. I get to spend twenty hours a day stuck in this cell with another guy. But I guess it's better than solitary confinement. At least here I can have my typewriter, and a few other luxuries I don't have if I were still in AdSeg. And I've only got 1,380 days left in prison. Then I'm out. One-thousand three-hundred eighty days . . . less than four years. I can do that standing on my head. After all, I did five in the dungeon.

August 3, 2004 What would I see if I could look into my own future? Five, ten, fifteen years from now? I'm not sure most people look that far down the road, either to plan or to predict. But I have. In fact, I've invested an extraordinary amount of time and energy into the process.

I do not like to "predict," per se, so I don't. Based on my troubled past I have difficulty predicting anything but more hardship, struggle, and failure. After all, who ever really changes?

So, instead of predicting, I choose to plan; or, if you will, to dream. I am not a pessimist at all. I am an optimist. I have a certain amount of confidence in my potential, though that confidence is tempered—maybe even nullified by the self-doubt and insecurity that are the legacy of my repeated and catastrophic failures. But there is something I feel inside that is even more powerful than either my confidence or my self-doubt. I intuitively feel that I have a purpose and a destiny in life that I will fulfill despite my personal weaknesses and failures.

Moreover, I have a concrete, detailed, and powerful vision of my future and my destiny, that I know will be realized if I can maintain my course and keep to my path. I call this vision my Big Dream.

This is difficult to write about, because it is something of a paradox. To realize my Big Dream I must see it and believe in it, even though it does not yet exist. Simply said, I must have faith where there is no just cause for faith. I must have hope, and optimism, where logic and rationality say none should be. I must believe in the impossible.

What is this Big Dream of mine? Do I dare share it with you? You might laugh and think me a fool and tell me what I already know—that it is impossible, unreasonable, absurd, ridiculous. Well, the truth is . . . I am a fool. I know this. It is what makes it possible for me to believe in the impossible so strongly that I can bring it to reality. So what will it hurt to tell you? Your ridicule will not be the first or last resistance I have encountered or will encounter. . . .

Dreaming Big in Prison

This then is my Big Dream: I dream that there can be a place in this world for dreamers and misfits. A place where lost souls can gather to find solace and comfort, acceptance and love, companionship and cooperation. Here they will commune in order to look within themselves to find answers to the question, "What is my purpose and path in this life?" And when they have answered that question they will ask others:

What am I capable of? What do I want? What will make me happy? What do I have to offer? How can I make the world a better place? How can I experience more love, more laughter, more satisfaction? How can I ease the suffering of others, and why would I want to? How can I transcend my limitations or increase my understanding? What is really important to me and how do I realize it in my life?

Here they will learn as well as teach the invaluable lesson that they truly have the power to shape their reality and create the future they want for themselves. That if they will only BE-LIEVE in, and SEE that which they desire, they can make it REAL.

Here they will work on their Art, their Music, their Dance, their Story, their own Big Dreams and Visions. They will have a place that provides them with a community of close and trusted friends, but also the solitude, freedom, and acceptance that are necessary for them to be themselves. They may even *find* themselves, or parts of themselves they would not have found had they not been given the opportunity to explore and experiment without fearing censure or rejection. And through this process they may learn how to love others without having to possess them or control them or tell them who to be or how to act or think. They might discover the joy and power of true unconditional love.

Here they will be able to make a living—not just survive, but prosper—while doing something they enjoy, and are good at, and can be proud of. Whatever gifts they have, they can offer up to their community and family who in turn will help complement those gifts and compensate for whatever weaknesses they are bound, as humans, to have.

Here they will live the truth that sex and sensuality and physical affection and carnal love are a beautiful, wonderful, necessary part of being human, and nothing to fear or hide or be ashamed of. Here there will be no things called sin or lust or perversion. Here there will only be Love in its many shapes and forms—and time enough to explore them all.

Here will be a Temple of the Eternal Groove. Here will be an Ashram and a Farm and a Center for the Healing Arts. Here will be Orchards and Woods and People Tending the Earth. Here will be Abundance and Opportunity and Possibility. Here will be Soft Falling Water and Pasture and the Laughter of Playing Children. Here will be Celebration and Hope and Thanksgiving.

Here will be Proof that a better world is possible.

Utopia on Earth

Here will be . . . Utopia.

If only such a place had existed when I was growing up. I think I wouldn't have had to spend fourteen years in prison. I think I wouldn't have had to spend so many of my childhood nights crying myself to sleep, not really understanding the how or why, but knowing that something was not right, and that I was missing something which would have been very good to have.

I think I would have not spent seven years of my early childhood and my adolescence in mental hospitals, strapped to beds or lying in cold empty cells. I think I would not have been a drug addict or a thief.

I think I would not have had to spend five straight years in the dungeon; five years without any human contact.

But then I think—if all those things had not been, then I would not be who I am. And if I had not been purified in the crucible of my torment and anguish and suffering, I might not know how important it is to have compassion, and how very special the little things are.

Surviving Rape in Prison

Michael J. Carlson

In this selection Michael J. Carlson describes how he was raped in prison and the impact of the crime on him. Carlson claims officials wrongly imprisoned him in a maximum-security unit in Amarillo, Texas, after a parole revocation hearing. He states that officials should not have placed him in the unit because the hearing officer never revoked his parole. While in the unit, Carlson alleges his cell mate raped him at knifepoint. After the rape, correctional officials released Carlson, but Carlson writes that he later violated his parole by leaving the halfway house to which corrections officials had assigned him because he feared that friends of the rapist who lived in the house would kill him. Officials returned him to prison, where he lives in fear of being raped again. He argues that the subsequent lax attitude of correctional officials in regard to pursuing prosecution of the rapist was cruel and inhumane punishment and violated his constitutional rights.

My name is Michael J. Carlson, and I am a 49 year [old] male bisexual currently incarcerated in Texas. My story is yet another Texas prison horror story of a rape that should never have happened, and the prevailing threat still in existence.

I was first brought back to Texas on February 19, 2005 for a parole revocation hearing, from Arizona, where I had been living on parole. That revocation hearing was held on March 7, 2005 at the Byrd Unit in Huntsville, Texas. After receiving all of the so-called "evidence", the hearing officer, Diane Corona, found I did not violate any condition of my parole, that I was to be reinstated and placed in a halfway house.

Michael J. Carlson, "Survivor Stories. Stop Prisoner Rape," www.spr.org, 2005. Reproduced by permission.

However, rather than sending me to a Pre-Release Prison, I was instead sent to the Bill Clements Unit, a maximum security prison in Amarillo, by TDCJ [Texas Department of Criminal Justice] and Parole Division officials. I should never have been placed on that unit or even reincarcerated, because my parole was not revoked, nor had I been convicted of any new felony offense, which, once I had been previously granted parole and released from prison, I could only be reincarcerated for.

On March 23, 2005 the Parole Board officially reinstated my parole, but kept me at the Bill Clements Unit.

No Steps Taken to Protect Me

I had repeatedly warned Warden [name omitted] that my physical safety was in grave danger in the unit, that because I was on parole, I was extremely vulnerable and at risk of being raped. Warden [name omitted] admitted that I wasn't supposed to be on his unit, and kept contacting parole officials to find out what they were going to do. But took no steps to protect me.

I had attempted to file grievances over my being assigned to the Bill Clements Unit when my parole had not been revoked and I had not been convicted of a new felony offense, and stated in each grievance that by assigning me to the Bill Clements Unit, prison and parole officials were clearly placing my safety in jeopardy, and again emphasized I was at risk of being raped. However, each time my grievances were returned to me, saying my complaints weren't "grievable issues".

On or about April 10th (or 11th), 2005, I was raped at knifepoint by my cellmate, [name omitted]. Although I reported the rape and asked for protection, nothing was done, and I was kept in that cell. I tried to get medical attention, but the nurse on duty refused to see me. Over the next 2 days I was raped repeatedly by [the cellmate]. On April 21st, 2005 I was finally released and sent to the CSC Halfway House in Fort Worth.

Crying Out for Help

When I arrived there on April 21st, 2005 I was extremely depressed and despondent, on the verge of commiting suicide. Not only was I struggling in trying to deal with the horror of having been raped at a maximum security prison I should never have been on, but I was also still having a difficult time in dealing with the murder of my beloved sister, who was murdered in Arizona on October 1, 2003. Her murder devastated me.

I was crying out for help, but no one, not even my parole officer, [name omitted], would help me. To make matters worse, friends of the inmate who raped me were also at the CSC Halfway House and had been threatening me. I was sinking deeper into my depression, and kept begging for help! But no one would listen. Finally, out of fear and desperation I walked away from that halfway house and hitchhiked back home to Tuscon [sic], Arizona on May 12, 2005.

On July 14, 2005 I was subsequently arrested in Tuscon on the parole violation warrant, and returned to Huntsville, Texas on August 18, 2005. . . . On September 6, 2005, the Texas Board of Pardons and Paroles revoked my parole, not even considering the living hell I was (and still am) going through when I left, and how all of my cries for help were ignored.

I have suffered the horror of being raped, a rape that should never have happened because I should never have been assigned to the Bill Clements Unit after having been found not guilty of any violation of my parole and being reinstated. TDCJ officials, Parole Division officials, and Warden [name omitted] are just as responsible for my being raped as [the cellmate] is.

Parole Revoked

As for my parole revocation now, yes, it was "wrong" for me to leave the CSC Halfway House and return to Arizona; I should have gone ahead and committed suicide instead, as I had first intended on doing. But it was also wrong for TDCJ and Parole officials to expose me to the repeated rape I suffered at a maximum security prison which they sent me to and kept me at even though they well knew I wasn't supposed to be on it. And it was just as wrong for my parole officer to refuse to help me; had she given that help I was begging for, I would never have left.

Rape is an inhumane crime against humanity, a horror no one should ever suffer through! It leaves psychological scars beyond repair, and now the Parole Board revokes my parole?!!

And now that the Parole Board has in fact unjustly revoked my parole, disregarding the hell and torment I've been through, I'm again at risk of being raped again!

Crime Against Humanity

What in fact has happened to me, and continues to happen, is a crime against humanity. It is cruel and inhumane treatment and punishment beyond description! These crimes against humanity must be stopped, and the conditions in Texas' prisons that breed them! Their lax attitude about them, and the predatory prisoners don't fear being "punished" by prison officials.

I don't want to see another prisoner suffer the horrors I've been through. Rapes such as mine occur all too frequently in Texas' prisons, with officials doing nothing to curtail them or prevent them. (How many inmates have they prosecuted for rape in prison?)

Because of this and my desire that no other Texas prisoner should suffer as I have, I have written this for everyone to read. I don't have anybody, no family, nothing, in the free world, or anybody to help me, and of course no attorney will help me pro bono. So I'm all alone.

The sad truth about all of this is that no one cares about it, wants to hear about it, or about the living hell and torment I've been through!

A Suicide in Prison

Jens Soering

In this excerpt Jens Soering, who is serving two life sentences for double murder, describes the suicide of a cell mate. He writes that his cell mate, Keith, ended up in prison because of charges of aggravated sexual assault on a minor. He liked his cell mate, who kept to himself, allowing Soering time to read, write, and pray. Soering writes that he blames himself for not practicing his belief that all sons of God are precious and for not noticing the signs of his cell mate's depression that led to his suicide. Soering also argues that terrible prison conditions can lead to hopelessness even for those not serving life imprisonments. When this article was published, Soering had served eighteen years of his life sentences. He is the author of two books, An Expensive Way to Make Bad People Worse: An Essay on Prison Reform from an Insider's Perspective *and* The Way of the Prisoner.

There is a chip in the paint on my bunk bed where Keith hanged himself. Like everything else in prison, penitentiary paint is cheap. Even a suicide's shoestring rope is enough to nick it. That scratch is all that is left of Keith now.

In the year or so that we shared a cell, Keith and I never really became friends. But this is not unusual. Prison life is not very conducive to genuine emotional bonding. To survive behind bars, you have to be constantly on your guard against the infinite variety of smiling manipulators. Years can pass before you accept another man as your "associate" or "stickman" and extend just a little trust to him. Even then, you never call him your "friend." In the penitentiary, that term is reserved for homosexual lovers.

So Keith and I lived side by side, or above one another in our bunk beds, in our 7-foot by 12-foot concrete box while remaining essentially strangers. Of course, we sometimes passed on prison gossip, discussed politics and shared brief memories of uncontroversial parts of our pasts. I learned, for instance, that Keith had betrayed his wife with an Indonesian woman while working overseas as a Navy contractor in the 1980's. But it was not until after his suicide that I found out why he had come to the penitentiary in the 1990's: for aggravated sexual battery on a minor.

What little I did come to know of Keith in our year together, I liked a lot. He took a shower every day; he always used headphones while watching his 5-inch TV; he did not steal from me; he did not try to rape me or start a consensual sexual relationship with me; he did not use drugs or brew homemade alcohol; he snored within reasonable limits; he kept quiet during my four daily centering prayer sessions, and he did not press conversation on me when I did not want it— which I never do. All this made Keith an ideal cellmate for me, a veritable gift from heaven. For all practical purposes, he was invisible, unnoticeable, absent.

Now, of course, he is truly and permanently absent. And I miss him.

Finding the Body

The last time I saw him alive was on April 27, 2004, at 6:10 a.m. I had performed centering prayer from 5 to 5:30 a.m., as I do every morning, and then read my Bible and wrote a letter. He got up once to urinate while I prayed, and his T-shirt very gently brushed my arm as he passed. Ten minutes after six, as I left the cell to go to breakfast, I saw him stirring on the bottom bunk, as if to rise and follow me. Just like every morning.

We had waffles that day, but I did not see Keith come through the chow line. So I left the dining hall early and returned to our housing unit to wake him up, to let him know that if he left immediately, he could still make it to breakfast before the chow line closed. I remember looking at my watch: it was 6:30 a.m. In a rush to ensure that Keith did not miss his waffles, I jerked open our cell door, and. . . .

The cell lights were off. Keith appeared to be sitting on the floor with his back against his bottom bunk, and I could see some blood on the front of his white T-shirt. I thought he had lost consciousness because of diabetic shock and then experienced a nose bleed.

According to what other inmates told me later, I shouted, "Oh my God!" I remember running to get the guard from the dayroom and returning with her to the cell. She was the one who turned on the light. And that is when we saw the white rope made of shoestrings, tied to my top bunk railing. Both of us could see immediately that Keith was dead.

Aftermath of a Suicide

After that, everything went crazy. Other inmates from surrounding cells, alerted by my initial shout, crowded around the open door to catch a glimpse of the dead guy. The guard I had brought to the cell was now also shouting "Oh my God" repeatedly, until someone pointed out to her that she really should radio for help. A few minutes later, some male guards arrived with a nurse, cut Keith down, and attempted C.P.R [cardiopulmonary resuscitation]. They tried very hard—I'll say that for them—but it was too late.

Meanwhile, still other guards had shepherded the other prisoners into their cells and put me in the now-empty dayroom. I watched them carry Keith past me on a stretcher. Then I just sat there for an hour or two.

Next came the inevitable interrogations: the institutional investigator, the assistant warden, an investigator from Virginia Department of Corrections headquarters, and finally a whole group that included all of the above plus a psychologist and a computer expert. "We think you know something you're not telling us," the assistant warden announced ominously. In the penitentiary, this is known as "squeezing my balls." Amazing how everything in prison has to be someone's fault, even a suicide.

Eventually, everyone appeared to agree that I was just as surprised and shocked as I appeared to be. So I was told that I could leave and that I should pack up Keith's property.

Of course, this was really the responsibility of two guards assigned to this task, but they were too scared to enter "the hangin' cell." With the help of another prisoner, I swept all of Keith's belongings into several enormous black trash bags, so the investigator could rummage through everything later—everything except Keith's Diet Cokes, that is. The other inmate kept all of those, as well as two bars of soap and a deodorant. Such is penitentiary life.

Questions of Why?

Perhaps I am no better. My first priority after packing Keith's property was to get a sponge, broom and mop bucket and remove any trace of him. That cell never got a cleaning as thorough as the one I gave it on the day of his death.

By then it was nighttime. So I took a shower, turned off the cell lights and climbed into my top bunk. Then I climbed back down, turned the small light on again and returned to bed. Sleeping alone in that cell with no lights at all was more than even I, with my 18 years of penitentiary experience and toughening-up, could stand.

The next morning, someone in authority must have figured out that I should not have been allowed to return to the cell and spend the night there. So I was told to pack up my own belongings and move into another cell for a week. Meanwhile "the hangin' cell" was officially, if belatedly, put "under investigation."

That investigation failed to turn up any clue as to why Keith took his life. According to the institutional investigator, who discussed this matter with the chief psychologist of the Department of Corrections, suicides who are truly determined to die neither signal their intentions beforehand nor leave any explanatory letters afterward. But among inmates and staff, of course, there was plenty of speculation.

The prison's computer class, where Keith had worked as a teacher's aide, had been the subject of an investigation in the week leading up to his death. One theory was that computer-generated child pornography had been found on the hard drive, and Keith had killed himself to escape the consequences. Because of the nature of the crime that had sent him to the penitentiary originally, the discovery of kiddie porn in his possession could conceivably have led to his civil commitment as a repeat sex offender upon completion of his current prison sentence in 2016. But one week after the suicide, the assistant warden assured me that child pornography had not in fact been found in the computer class or anywhere else.

More Theories

Another theory was that Keith had sought admittance to this prison's innovative Sex Offender Residential Treatment (SORT) program, a nationally recognized success. Under the current correctional regime, however, he would have had to serve another full decade behind bars before he could enter SORT in the last two years prior to his scheduled release. Wanting to change yourself is not enough to earn a second chance—not any more. But Keith read newspapers and thus was aware of the political realities affecting prisoners, so he could hardly have been surprised by the complete merciless-ness of the system.

So in the end, what the few of us who liked Keith are left with is a mystery. He wanted out, a sentiment all of us under-stand, and he found a way. What many of the rest of us have been asking ourselves is why we are not following Keith's way of making parole. No one wants to say this out loud, of course. But I can see it in the slumped shoulders, and I hear it in the joking advice to "keep hangin' in there, buddy." Was Keith a kind of penitentiary prophet, showing us all some ugly truths about our own lives?

In the housing unit where he and I lived, there are many inmates who will most likely die behind bars—lifers who will never be released. Currently 127,677 prisoners are serving life sentences in this country's state and federal penitentiaries, one out of every 11 inmates. In the federal system and six states, lifers are officially ineligible for parole, but even in those states whose laws technically still allow the release of such prisoners, parole grants are virtually unheard of for those serving life.

The comparatively small penitentiary where I am housed holds at least two men who have spent over 40 years behind bars, several with more than 30 under their belts, and literally dozens in the "20-plusyears" club. With only 18 years of incarceration—almost half my life—I am actually considered a "fresh fish" around here.

Regrets About Keith

But we lifers, we are the dead. Our executions may be stretched out over four or five decades, but in the end, life without parole produces exactly the same result as lethal injection: 127,677 human beings killed by their government.

All of us lifers know this, yet for some reason we are not the ones who kill ourselves. Keith, a man who actually had a firm release date, albeit 12 years from now, is the one who committed suicide. Why? I do not know.

I do know that I wish I had listened to Keith, even to his silence. So much of my life now is spent on centering prayer, the prayer of inner silence, that I was grateful to have a taciturn cellmate like Keith. Someone mature enough to keep quiet, watch his television without bothering me, and let me do my praying and writing. Someone who did not need a babysitter. So I failed to be my brother's keeper. Admittedly, Keith seems not to have wanted someone to talk him out of hanging himself. But the fact is that I never even tried.

When I turn to my Bible as I struggle with Keith's suicide, I find two passages that shed at least some light on his death: the stories of Samson and the so-called "bad thief."

You will recall that thanks to Delilah, Samson was finally captured by the Philistines, "bound . . . with bronze fetters [and] put to grinding in the prison" (Jgs 16:21). On one occasion, while being taunted in the great hall by "about three thousand men and women [for their] amusement," he pushed down the columns and "killed at his death . . . more than he had killed during his lifetime" (Jgs 16:30). So Scripture tells us, anyway.

Hopelessness Kills

As a prisoner myself, I can recognize another prisoner's fantasy. There is not an inmate alive who has not dreamed of ending his own pain in a grand final gesture and taking as many of his captors with him to the grave as possible. Whoever wrote the story of Samson's suicide was perhaps a convict himself, and he expressed a very important and sad truth about life in the penitentiary: hopelessness kills. I am sure that Keith would have pushed down the columns of the great hall if he could have. But in the end, even this satisfaction was denied him. And that would have only added to his hopelessness.

The other Bible passage that has given me at least a little perspective on Keith's death is the description of the "bad thief" at Jesus' crucifixion. Traditionally, Christians focus on the good thief, the repentant one—that symbol of mercy in extremis. But most of America's 127,677 lifers, and almost certainly my cellmate Keith, identify more closely with the bad thief, the one who died without hope and with curses on his lips (Lk 23:39).

Much like modern-day jailbirds, the bad thief had probably learned that central rule of prison life with which I began: do not let anyone get close to you! An occasional "associate" or "stickman" is acceptable—but no "friends," please. Trust no one! Especially not some nutcase on the cross next to yours who claims he is the Son of God. Yeah, sure, buddy—and I'm the Shah of Iran. Let me do my time, and you do yours. And keep the noise down, will ya!

That is how I lived while sharing a cell with Keith: I failed to recognize him as a child of God. The light eternal, the light that shone before the creation of the universe, this light was flowing through Keith every single day that we were cellmates, and I did not see it. God's beloved son was in the bunk bed below mine, but I was too busy praying and writing to pay attention.

"This is how all will know that you are my disciples: if you love one another," Jesus said at the Last Supper (Jn 13:35). I was a poor disciple, and I am sorry. May God have mercy on Keith's soul—and also on mine.

Inside Canada's Federal Prisons for Women

Ann Hansen

Ann Hansen is a former federal prisoner in Canada who has testified to the Canadian Human Rights Commission about her experience in the prison system. In this selection Hansen describes what life in prison was like for her and for current female prisoners. She writes that the women live in inhumane conditions in cramped cells located in segregated wings within men's maximum-security prisons. The women prisoners, many of whom are victims of sexual abuse, also live in constant fear of a violent uprising of the male inmates. Despite more than fifty government investigations since the 1930s into the conditions that women endure in Canada's prison facilities, little has changed. Hansen argues that society must do more to help these women and reform the women's prison system.

Hansen was sentenced to life in prison in July 1984 but was paroled in seven years. She was sentenced for her involvement with the leftist underground group, Direct Action—also known as the Squamish Five. The group received national attention in 1982 when they bombed the Litton Systems Plant in protest of the company's role in arms production. Hansen now works with the group Womyn4Justice, which she and a number of ex-prisoners founded on Prison Justice Day, August 10, 2002. Since its founding, the Kingston, Ontario–based group has worked to raise public awareness about prison abolition and the conditions facing women prisoners in Canada.

[Editor's note: The abbreviation P4W stands for Prison for Women, a federal women's prison located in Kingston, Ontario. The facility closed in 2000 and was replaced by the cur-

Ann Hansen, "Prisons Are the Looking-Glass of Society: The Struggle Towards Dignity for Women (Federal Prisons for Women)," in *Canadian Dimension*, vol. 36, September–October 2002. Reproduced by permission of the author.

rent system of housing maximum-security women prisoners within segregated wings of men's maximum-security prisons. The government has also recently built six regional prisons for women. These prisons have minimum to medium security.]

The history of federal women prisoners is riddled with scathing reports and condemnations of their prison conditions and yet, to my knowledge, the situation for women prisoners in Canada has not changed since P4W was first described as "unfit for bears" by the Archambault Royal Commission, four years after the first women were moved there from Kingston Penitentiary (KP) in 1934. By 1990, the Task Force on Federally Sentenced Women was the fiftieth federal report to chronicle the inadequacies of prison conditions and programs for women. I became personally aware of the repetitive nature of history in January [2002], when I attended a Canadian Human Rights Commission conference to once again document "cases of discriminatory treatment of" federally sentenced women (FSW) in preparation for a government brief. During this conference, I became aware that the same Commission had condemned the Corrections Service of Canada (CSC) for discriminatory treatment of FSW in a government report back in 1981. I ask myself, why does the government continue to waste money on report after report that condemns prison conditions, recommends improvements and then refuses to act upon these recommendations?

I was a federally sentenced prisoner from 1983 until 1990 and will be on parole for the rest of my life. During the latest Human Rights Commission conference, I was asked to testify about my experiences in the prison system. Since I had been out of prison for 12 years, I decided to contact a few women I knew still inside the federal prisons to compare how much prison conditions had changed since I had been released on full parole. I must admit, I wasn't shocked by their testimony, but my cynicism regarding prison reform became even more grounded in reality than ever before.

In 1983, most women serving life sentences were transferred to P4W as maximum-security prisoners to do their time along with medium- and minimum-security prisoners. As maximum-security prisoners, we lived in a population of roughly 100 women who moved about freely from work to their ranges or wings and the yard. There were jobs available for all security levels although they were menial and certainly did not prepare the women for employment on the street, but at that time it was possible to take university courses or upgrade one's education in the prison school. Other than Alcoholics Anonymous, I can't recall any treatment programs for drug and alcohol addiction, and there was one psychologist who specialized in sexual-abuse counselling. It might not seem like much, but in the evenings and weekends, we could paint and decorate our cells to reflect our personal identities and could associate in common rooms, play sports in a full-size gym, work out in a weightroom, or jog in a fairly large, open prison yard. When a maximum-security prisoner became a medium-security prisoner, not much changed, but there was the possibility of moving to the wing, an area somewhat like a dorm, with unlocked cell doors and windows in each cell.

By the time a prisoner cascaded to minimum, it was possible to get the odd institutional group pass to go swimming at Artillery Park, or even be transferred to the Isabel McNeil House, a minimum-security house across the road from P4W. At the minimum, women could work in the community, live in a house without security fencing, could cook their own meals and generally take on the responsibilities of normal life.

Finally a prisoner could apply for day parole at the Elizabeth Fry Detweiler House in Kingston, which also served as a place where women could stay while on passes. Although this may sound idyllic to proponents of capital punishment and the concept of prison as retribution—in reality, prison conditions and programs in the eighties were so inadequate that the overwhelming effect was one of punishment.

Scenes of Degradation

P4W's final death knell came in 1994 when a murky black-and-white video that resembled a low-budget pornography film was aired across the country on the evening news showing the male riot squad in full facial masks stripping female prisoners of their clothes with scissors against their will in the segregation cells of P4W. These scenes of degradation had taken place after the prisoners had already been locked in the segregation cells following a confrontation with female guards. Even though most federal women prisoners can recount equally horrific experiences, the public was shocked to learn that these grainy porno scenes were real T.V. taped directly inside Canada's modern prison system. The government responded predictably by setting up another commission, headed by Justice Louise Arbour to investigate and then make recommendations into what was officially described in terms that could only serve to downplay the crisis: "An Inquiry into Certain Events at P4W."

Two weeks after having their clothes cut off by male prison guards, the six women involved were involuntarily transferred to a segregated range in KP, a prison noted for taking the unwanted sex offenders from the other men's maximum-security penitentiaries. The women were eventually transferred back to P4W after arguing successfully among other things to the Ontario Court that they had histories of being sexually abused by men and did not feel safe in KP. Many months of testimony and thousands of dollars later, to no one's surprise, Justice Arbour's commission recommended that P4W be closed and, once again in its characteristically understated way, concluded that "there is, if nothing more, an appearance of oppression in confining women in an institution which will inevitably contain a large number of sexual offenders. This is particularly true of the Regional Treatment Centre [KP]." More troublesome, in my opinion, is the fact that the placement of a small group of women in a male prison effectively precludes their interaction with the general population of that institution. If transfer inevitably means segregation, the decision to transfer should take into account the limitations on the permissible use of administrative segregation.

What's It Like?

Despite the Ontario Court General Division, the Arbour Commission and the CS's own correctional investigator, here we are in June, 2002, with small groups of women prisoners being confined in virtual segregation within men's maximum-security penitentiaries—namely Springhill Institution in Nova Scotia, the Regional Reception Centre in Quebec, the Saskatchewan Penitentiary in Prince Albert and the Regional Psychiatric Centre in Saskatoon. These women's maximum-security units share strikingly common denominators, each unit has a population ranging from one to 12 women who are kept in virtual isolation from the general men's population— they have either limited or no access to work, recreation, or treatment programs. Life in these women's units bears more of a resemblance to that of special-handling units designed for men who have killed guards or other prisoners than it does to that in a general prison population. Theoretically, at least, these women are being held in these units because they are maximum-security prisoners, not for special punishment.

The situation in Saskatchewan Penitentiary is typical of life for a woman as a maximum-security prisoner. You would be placed in an open-barred cell similar to the kind you see in stereotypical Hollywood films, on a small range with three or four other women. No matter how many layers of paint they apply, nothing can erase the haunting thoughts that plague you, knowing that this used to be the men's psychiatric unit, and nothing can stop you from contemplating the fact that you share more in common with Canada's first three female prisoners in 1835 than with any free women in the 21st century.

Every day of your life you wake up to the clanging of the metal doors unlocking, opening up your cell to the same two or three other women with whom you will share a tiny common space for many years. There are five other ranges just like yours in this unit but you won't get to associate with the two or three women in each of these, nor with the 500 men who live in the rest of the penitentiary around you.

And you pray at night when you hear loud mysterious noises that those 500 men are not in the midst of a riot progressing rapidly towards your unit. Let's face it, can anyone think of a men's maximum-security prison that has not had a major riot? I can't. And I can't think of a men's maximum-security prison that doesn't have some sexual predators either openly or covertly prowling its ranges. Considering that you are one of the 80 per cent of all federal women prisoners who have been sexually abused, you are not always comfortable being escorted through the men's areas to and from the few activities available. But at the same time you feel like you are going to either explode or implode if you have to spend another day in that small space with the same two or three people. Your meals are even delivered onto the tiny range from the men's area and you share a shower with the same two or three women. Inevitably tension builds. And you find small consolation in the words of the correctional investigator condemning your situation as "unacceptable and discriminatory" even for prisoners.

Wasted Studies Lead to Little Change

Every time there is a crisis within the prison system, the government diverts the anger of society and its need for a resolution into some government commission, inquiry, or report. They began in P4W, just four years after the prison opened, with the Archambault Royal Commission. Since 1968 no less than 13 government studies and private-sector reports have reaffirmed that P4W should be closed. In 1978, when Solicitor

General Jean-Jacques Blais announced that the prison would be closed within a year, instead, he turned around and built a new, 18-foot-high concrete wall. Then again in 1990 a federal task force recommended the closure of P4W, an occasion which Solicitor General Pierre Cadieux used to pronounce the imminent construction of five new, regional prisons for women at a cost of $50 million. Both the wall and the closure of P4W are good examples of how recommendations by commissions, inquiries and reports are invariably transformed into more prisons, more security and more prisoners.

At the latest Human Rights Commission conference I was surprised to learn that the Canadian Charter of Human Rights and Freedoms, as well as the Universal Declaration of Human Rights, applied to prisoners. I think my surprise was based on the incredible gulf that exists between these rights in theory and their application in reality. If I hadn't experienced first-hand just how vacant the promise of human rights is in prison, I would be the first person to suggest that perhaps all the good-intentioned recommendations of the various government commissions could be implemented through legal pressure to have prisoners' rights upheld. But unfortunately I know all too well how much of a mirage those prisoners' rights really are. Ask the women in Saskatchewan Penitentiary about "freedom of assembly" about which even the CSC states, "inmates are entitled to reasonable opportunities to assemble peacefully and associate with other inmates within the penitentiary, subject to reasonable limits as are prescribed for protecting the security of the penitentiary or the safety of persons." Ask any prisoner about freedom of speech. Charges stemming from arguing with guards are systemic. Ask prisoners anywhere about freedom of religion. Unless a prisoner is Catholic or Protestant, there are few religious or spiritual "leaders" who have access to prisoners to guide people in their traditional ceremonies. Ask prisoners about freedom of the press. When I was released I was sent a box full of magazines, newspaper articles and books I had never even been notified of being denied. And, of course, federal prisoners can't vote. The list of freedoms and rights that is not applicable to prisoners is too vast to expand upon in this article.

The Women in Prisons Are Victims

So why should we care about what happened to those women in P4W, anyway? Prison is the looking-glass of society. It reflects what the values and characteristics of our society are. What do we see through the looking-glass? We see women who are the most victimized people in our society. They are the poorest, least educated and most racially discriminated against. They have been physically and sexually abused at the hands of their own fathers and mothers, and then deserted by the fathers of their children. Is this just political rhetoric, you ask? The numbers paint the picture, I answer. Half of FSW have a grade-nine or lower education; 40 per cent are illiterate; the majority were unemployed at the time of their crime; even though Native people make up two per cent of the population, they are 25 per cent of the FSW; two-thirds are single mothers and 80 per cent have histories of sexual or physical abuse. And, even when women do commit violent crimes, 62 per cent are classified as common assault and the majority of those convicted of murder have killed a spouse or partner who they reported as having physically or sexually abused them.

No matter how I look at it, the women in prison are the victims of the inequities, injustices and discrimination within our society. Without prisons as a social-control mechanism, the poor would take back what is rightfully theirs; the rebellious would no longer obey laws they know are unjust; and revolutionaries would win the just war. Execution is the only social-control mechanism more effective than prison.

Don't Ignore the Plight of Women Prisoners

If only I could say the solution was reform and the struggle for prisoners' rights, but unfortunately the contradictions within the capitalist economic system make these solutions illusory. To pursue prisoners' rights is somewhat akin to a heat-weary traveller in the desert trudging endlessly towards a shimmering mirage over sand dune after sand dune. No matter how close the traveller gets to the oasis mirage, just as it seems within reach, it disappears over the next rise. Is this not what has happened with the closure of P4W? The prisoners were promised better prison conditions. Now we see women in tiny units inside men's prisons, and the mediums and minimums are living in small, regional prisons with few treatment or educational programs. The government claims there are too few women prisoners spread out across the country to make programs cost-effective. Yet millions of dollars have been spent on converting ranges in men's prisons into segregated women's units.

Despite the seemingly hopeless task of improving prison conditions, we can't just turn our backs and walk away from the women and men in prison. It's important to try to help them, even if the gains are few and far between. Certainly even what may seem like a small improvement is a big improvement for someone in prison.

So what is the key to solving this contradiction between working for prisoners' rights and living within a capitalist economy where prisons are an essential social control mechanism? I believe that Claire Culhane, who died in 1996 after devoting the better part of her life to abolishing prisons while fighting for prisoners' rights, had found the key to unlock this puzzle. It is found in the simple words she inscribed on the letterhead of her Prisoners' Rights Group: "We can't change prisons without changing society. We know that this is a long and dangerous struggle. But the more who are involved in it, the less dangerous, and the more possible it will be."

Prison Guards, Staff, and Volunteers

The Joys of Teaching in Jail

Lynn Olcott

In this excerpt Lynn Olcott describes her experience as a General Educational Development (GED) teacher in the Incarcerated Education Program sponsored by the Syracuse (New York) City School District and the Onondaga County Sheriff's Office. She writes of the contrast between her students in jail and her well-off suburban high school students. The students in jail, she argues, are hungry for knowledge and want to make a better life for themselves once they leave jail. Olcott states that she enjoyed the experience of teaching in jail so much she would rather teach there than in a suburban high school where students do not have the same zeal for learning. Olcott is a freelance writer and English teacher living in Homer, New York. She is also an adjunct professor in the Foundations and Social Advocacy Department at the State University of New York at Cortland.

I want to go back to jail. I'm serious. I was a more honest, more effective teacher there. I trusted my students, and they trusted me. We worked together toward the next scheduled GED (General Educational Development) test and filled ourselves with as much literature as I could put in their willing hands. Every day I went deep into a maximum-security facility to the women's pod, where my students lived and ate and studied. Every day I encountered students who were eager to learn and glad for the simple materials I brought. I rediscovered pure, joyous teaching. In that stark environment, I rediscovered the educational power of kindness and respect.

Like so many of us now, I was a card-carrying member of the "sandwich generation," caregiver for my father while I still had a teenager at home. When my father died, I was exhausted, sad, and thoroughly disillusioned with long-term care, Medicare, and every other kind of care. I was eager to return to teaching, my late father's profession as well as mine. I responded to an ad in the paper looking for a teacher for an incarcerated education program, with no real idea of what that meant. My father's funeral was on a stormy Friday in January. The next week, I was thrilled to be hired as a GED teacher at the Onondaga County Justice Center [in New York]. My new life had begun.

From the very beginning, I was struck by the contrast between the bleak correctional environment and the rich educational experiences offered there. The offerings were not limited to GED courses but included training in office technology, anger management, food service, and many other subjects. The Syracuse City School District, in conjunction with the Onondaga County Sheriff's Office, has operated the Incarcerated Education Program for several years. It is a "showcase program" in that it is well respected in corrections services circles. But it is practically unknown to the general public, even in the county where it exists. The Justice Center houses about 600 prisoners at any one time, and perhaps 60 or 70 of them are women. It is a nonsentenced facility, so students might be in the program for a few days or a few months before being bailed out, sentenced upstate, or transferred to other facilities. The GED test is given in-house about every two months. Pass rates, about 50%, equal and sometimes exceed those on the "outside."

In New York State, inmates aged 16 through 21 who lack a GED or high school diploma are required to attend classes. Many students over 21 attend voluntarily. Most of the girls and women I met were African American and had left school around 10th grade, usually due to pregnancy or childbirth. Most were incarcerated for economic crimes—prostitution, shoplifting, passing bad checks, selling drugs, and occasionally burglary and assault. Most scored between the fourth- and sixth-grade levels on the TABE (Test of Adult Basic Education), the test we used as a baseline. Most were involved with men who never came to see them. Most had children, whom they missed very much, being cared for by relatives.

A Self-Appointed Assistant

The first student I met was Sally. She was about 40 years old, and her children were being raised by her father and step-mother. Several acts of violence had brought her here and to prison in the past. Sally instantly became my self-appointed assistant and made it her priority to have the heavy tables dragged together and the shaky whiteboard erected and ready for us every morning. She worked hard and encouraged the other students with persuasive personal lectures on the importance of education. When she left to serve time in a state prison, I missed her.

Sally's close friend Sheryl took over the role of encourager, but she left the moving of the heavy tables to the kids. I usually had eight or 10 students at a time, of different ages and working at different levels. I invented a simple, individualized system that students could enter easily and could use to track their own achievements. I taught math, science, and social studies as well as language arts. I liked the diversity of subject matter and was grateful for my own liberal arts education. Though technically I taught this medley of subjects, I was primarily a teacher of remedial reading and writing, a teacher of reading comprehension, a teacher of guerrilla English.

Teaching writing was fascinating. My students had a great deal to write about. Sheryl wrote about living in the South and about how her family had made a living picking cotton before coming north with her brave mother and cruel stepfather. Tina wrote a moving essay about wanting to gather her scattered family and cook Sunday dinner for them. A tough high school girl named Ilene wrote an amazing piece of irony about stolen watches and doing time. I was not really teaching writing at all; I was merely opening the drawstrings on bags of experiential treasure. What I was teaching—to students who had not written 250 words together in decades, if ever—was the format expected in a successful GED essay.

Prisoners' Fierce Eagerness to Learn

At the request of one of the high school girls, we read Sophocles' play *Antigone*. The students argued fiercely and eloquently over the judgment of King Creon against Antigone, who insisted on honoring her dead brother. Later we read parts of *Romeo and Juliet*. The students' soft ghetto voices gave the Elizabethan speech a powerful new music. Their favorite play was *A Raisin in the Sun*, by Lorraine Hansberry. We all knew people like Lena, the matriarch, and her weak, handsome son, from our own lives. We read excerpts from *Inside the Brain*, by Ronald Kotulak. One student traced her own learning difficulties to her mother's drug use during pregnancy. Another took heart at the awesome resilience of the adult brain, feeling that it was possible for her to master math and pass the GED, though the work was very hard for her. She had not stayed in school long enough to learn algebra, and this was a real disadvantage for GED students.

In quiet moments, I would look out on the tables of students and admit undeniably that these were the kids (whatever their ages) that we had failed to reach. These are kids we all had in our classes, kids who were often behavior problems, kids who had a hard time with learning, either because of circumstances or brain wiring or both. We passed or failed them, or we placed them elsewhere and forgot about them. They quit school, but they did not go away. I felt like Alice, stepping through the looking glass of American education and meeting firsthand these tales of almost incomprehensible woe.

Some days at the GED table were heartbreaking. There was Lily, who sometimes had to excuse herself from class, eyes brimming with tears, because the image of her teenage son, lying dead of a gunshot wound, was still too raw. Her own drug use could only intermittently obscure the pain. There was Ellie, just 18, who braided her own hair into shining French braids and who had been incarcerated one way or another since she was 10. There were girls and women with scars and burn marks and injured eyes. There were girls and women who had had their front teeth knocked out. Some were safer in jail than at home. Every day when I left the jail, I took a deep breath of fresh air, but my students were locked away, and their stories and their anguish and their unique female rage were locked away with them.

I have great respect for the deputies in the residence pods. I just came in every morning with my case of GED materials and enjoyed a few hours of pure and joyful teaching. It was the deputies who handled the round-the-clock despair of incarcerated lives.

Winter ripened into spring. My students left for prison, or for rehab, or for home, and there were new students almost every day. I could no longer support my family on the part-time salary, and we needed health insurance. Dutifully I applied for every full-time English teaching job within commuting distance from home. I am sure that I bombed more than one interview just by being too enthusiastic about jail! On the last day of summer before school started, I was hired for a long-term English substitute position in a suburban high school an hour from home. I would be able to make ends meet again, with the family insured. My father would approve. Or would he? I could not shake the feeling that, in terms of my calling as a teacher, I was selling out. I was abandoning students who needed me for students who probably didn't.

My new students are well dressed and college-bound. They have jet skis and cellphones, and if they ever get into trouble, it is unlikely that they will have to rely on a court-appointed attorney—or even need to know what one is. I do not have a classroom. But what am I complaining about? I have a cart that I take from room to room. In the jail, I lugged around a plastic case. Maybe it is the role of substitute that makes me feel tentative. Maybe it is the constant interruptions, the reminders about "crazy sock" day, the announcements about senior baby pictures, and the grade-level fund-raisers. Maybe I just want to go back to jail.

Recently I got a letter from Sally. She is doing one to three years at "Miss Betty's House," the insider's term for the Bedford Hills Correctional Facility. She tells me she is attending GED classes again, determined to pass this time. She says she will never give up, and I believe her. She thanks me for encouraging her to write. She reminds me that I always told the students that the world will be a better place when more women tell their stories. She says she plans to put her life down in a book someday, and I believe she will.

I miss the dull roar of electric doors closing behind me. I miss the courage of the students who came to the GED table ready to learn, despite broken lives, despite deep worries and uncertain futures. I miss the sense that I am somehow making it up to them for our educational failures of the past. Sure, I know it is a drop in the bucket. But I also know that each day, as I went deeper into the experiences of these women, I came closer to students who honored me with their willing minds. Each day in the jail, I was true to my calling. In jail I was a teacher.

Correction Officers Can Make a Difference

C. Shawn Sapriken

In this selection C. Shawn Sapriken writes that he became a correctional officer because he believes in the cause of restorative justice. Proponents of restorative justice believe that only violent career criminals should be imprisoned, while nonviolent offenders should be sentenced to work in closely monitored community projects to earn money to make financial restitution to their victims and their victims' families, to repay court and corrections costs, and to support their own families. Sapriken argues that imprisoning nonviolent criminals is not effective in producing societal change. He states that he chose to work in corrections in the hope of encouraging nonviolent offenders to change their lives and not commit more crimes once they are released from prison. When Sapriken wrote this article, he had completed his first two years as a federal correctional officer in Alberta, Canada.

I grew up with a couple of correctional employees for neighbors and family friends. They have worked for the Correctional Service of Canada (CSC) for more than 20 years, and though they tried their best to discourage me from following them into a career in federal corrections, they failed miserably. They told me I would likely become jaded and develop a cynical view of the entire criminal justice system and with humanity in general, like so many who work on the front line of CSC. But even as they warned me, they inadvertently revealed what I saw as a career with the potential for amazing opportunities, and I could not help but ignore their counsel.

I have heard a career as a correctional employee in Canada described as 30 years of mind-numbing boredom and 30 minutes of heart-stopping terror. Only halfway into the second year of my own career, I can already attest to the boredom. And no one wishes for it, but there are also those occasions when correctional employees face the real danger of not going home to their families.

Unlike police officers, correctional officers are rarely armed, and they must work rather diligently to ensure that neither are their charges—an act of self-preservation more than anything. Where the police have the task of tracking and arresting offenders, correctional employees must interact with these offenders on a round-the-clock basis in jails that resemble the dungeons of medieval Europe. Police are respected and lionized for their work—and rightly so. Correctional officers, however, are often misunderstood and viewed as little better than those they guard. Thirty years ago, according to one of my college instructors, the requirements for prospective correctional employees in Alberta included having little more than a high school diploma, being over 6 feet tall and hopefully having high school football experience because brawls with offenders were a daily occurrence. It was said that the difference between the keepers and the kept was what side of the bars they were on.

So, why would anyone choose such a potentially dangerous and thankless profession? For a great many reasons, I assure you, but it is not a choice for those who cannot embrace the concepts of humanism and restorative justice.

A Belief in Restorative Justice

Absolutely no one can do anything to change or prevent a crime that has already been committed. What we in the law enforcement field can do—and what I believe is incumbent upon every one of us in that field to do—is make every effort to prevent an offender from committing another offense. And prison, though a very attractive deterent for all of us with thoughts of retribution, simply does not work. What prison often does well is teach inmates how to be better offenders and hardens them in a ruthless and survivalist environment. It also can slowly divest an individual of the ability to think and act responsibly for one's self. After years of being told when to eat, sleep, wake, what to do and how to do it, how effective do you think that individual will be as a law-abiding citizen, expected to make his or her own choices? Furthermore, it is an incredible drain on Canadian taxpayers. It costs Canadian taxpayers nearly 80,000 Canadian dollars per year to maintain each and every male federal offender in prison. With a national inmate population of about 15,000, that is a lot of wasted money—to the tune of more than $9 billion per year, every year. And the cost is only going up.

Prison can also be just as hard on the correctional employee; it is said by the Canadian correctional services industry that they, too, serve a life sentence—they just get paid better. Imagine having to drive to work, shift work, in a nondescript car because you do not want to risk having an offender be released from prison and recognize your car while you are on a family picnic at the park. You wear a $10 watch because you do not want your nice one stolen or broken. You work in a concrete building with shatterproof windows and lit mainly by fluorescent bulbs in tamper-resistant casings. You are constantly abused verbally by dozens of offenders who would not hestitate to hurt you as soon as they look at you. But that is all part of the job, right? Yes, but it does have a profound effect on the worker. Defense and coping mechanisms become a part of the routine and one becomes hardened, jaded and cynical, which is precisely what those neighbors of mine were trying to keep me from.

A Need to Do More

I am 6 feet 3 inches tall. I have a high school diploma. And I not only played football, but rugby as well. Thankfully, this is not what qualifies me to work in corrections. I also have a

Corrections guards are often thought of as serving a "life sentence" along with the prisoners they guard. AP Images

college education in corrections that was founded on the concept of restorative justice and on the idea that in order to reduce the recidivism rate in Canada, we need to do more than just cage our offenders. They will be let out one day and I, for one, would prefer they knew something more than how to be a better predator.

It is easy to see why a correctional employee can become cynical, and very easy to sympathize with the idea that "once a con, always a con." The challenge is in seeing the possibility for something better and working to achieve it. And that is why I chose to work in this profession; not to fall into the excuses and cynical attitudes that offenders are inherently evil and beyond hope, nor to work in a prison—prisons are ineffective, ultimately more harmful than good and a colossal waste of money. In my opinion, I choose to maintain a positive outlook and accept the challenge to make every effort to protect the public and assist every offender I can to become a law-abiding citizen because I believe in the potential to succeed at it. Naive? Possibly. The wide-eyed, take-on-the-world ravings of a young newcomer to the field? Maybe. But then, those are the kinds of cynical viewpoints I intend to shun. I do not expect to be thanked for my efforts, but then, that is not why I ignored the counsel of my family friends in the first place.

A Day in the Life of a Prison Guard in Training

Ted Conover

In his book New Jack Guarding Sing Sing, *Ted Conover, an undercover journalist who took a job as a prison guard at Sing Sing, gives a firsthand account of his often nerve-racking work in this major New York federal prison. In this selection excerpted from his book, Conover describes some of his experiences at Sing Sing. He writes of an emergency on the wing for which he had charge of the keys, which is a crucial responsibility in a prison. He dropped the keys in the chaos of the moment, but a more experienced guard covered for him. Conover also details another incident in which an inmate stole food from the cafeteria. The senior guard Conover was working with wanted to cover up the incident and divvy up the food among all the inmates on the wing because the guard was afraid of them, Conover writes. Conover's book was selected as a Pulitzer Prize finalist and won the 2001 National Book Critics Circle Award.*

Keys were power. And they were responsibility—because many, many bunglings could be traced back to a set of keys and the person who had been entrusted with them. When to lock and when to unlock was, by one reckoning, what we were here to learn. "You are never wrong, in prison, to lock a gate," a sergeant had reassured us at lineup one day. But it was more complicated than that. Gates had to be unlocked for the prison to function smoothly—and then, at the right moment, to be locked again. Sing Sing was a place of, probably, over two thousand locks, many with the same key. The cardinal sin, the one thing you were never, ever to do, was lose your keys. A lost key could fall into inmates' hands. A lost key was a disaster.

I was back in B-block a few days later, responsible for half of Q-gallery, on the flats, as well as the center gate—the main access point from the flats to the galleries above. To learn this job, I had to handle the keys. But while the regular officer, a fat, powerful-looking cigar chomper named Orrico, was at pains to explain the job, he was not handing me the ring of keys. Instead, he played with them, twirled them around a big finger, caught them in his meaty palm. There were several, I could see: the cell key, the brake-padlock key, a gym-door key or two, an end-gate key, a center-gate key, a fire-alarm key, and at least one other, all of them different. The pewter-colored cell key was the biggest, its shaft as thick as a Mont Blanc pen, with a silver dollar-sized handle at one end and skeleton key-like chiselings in a tab at the other.

Red-Dot Emergency Procedures

In case of a red-dot emergency, Orrico was saying, I was to get to the center gate as soon as possible. It was the main passage to the upper floors, and I would need to let through all the officers who had to pass, then lock it back up. In no case was I to follow the responding red-dot officers upstairs—even if my best friend worked up there, even if I heard officers screaming out in agony—because control over the gate was essential to the block's security.

Concluding his lecture, Orrico left to pursue a cup of coffee and handed me the keys. No sooner had he disappeared than the red-dot alarm sounded. Officers were dashing toward the center gate, arriving before me. I rushed through them to open the gate, then realized I had no idea which key to use. My heart rate soared as I stood there fumbling with the key ring while more and more officers shouted at me to hurry up. "Somebody just take it!" I heard someone say.

I had just stuck the right key into the lock when the officers disappeared behind me. The alarm wasn't upstairs, they'd realized, but through the short passage, to V-gallery. I peered around the corner and saw them massing in two huge piles, evidently on top of inmates. Then *bang bang bang* —on the center gate again. This time, officers were on the other side of it, responding from upstairs. Among them was my classmate Don Allen. "Come on, Conover, let's go!" he yelled excitedly. I found the key again. I turned it. A second flood of officers pushed by me.

A few minutes later, everyone was back on his feet, including three mashed-looking inmates, who were handcuffed behind their backs. Each inmate had an officer holding the chain of his cuffs and marching him back to my gallery. First came a young black man with some swelling over his brow and a lot of blood flowing down the left side of his face. Next was a long-haired Latino with no shirt. Finally, there was another young black man, bleeding from gashes around the temple. They were to be locked in empty shower stalls on Q-gallery, and for that they needed keys.

Dropping the Keys

Orrico appeared. "Where are they?" he demanded, holding out his open palm. I checked my belt. They weren't there! I looked in the center-gate keyhole—not there either. My heart sank. "What?" Orrico demanded loudly. "You don't have them?" This was the cardinal sin. Orrico called out to the milling officers, "Anybody got the center-gate key?" From the throng of officers came some questioning looks. Finally, Don Allen emerged holding—God bless him—my keys. Orrico snatched them away in disgust.

"You dropped them," Allen said quietly. I had no idea how it had happened. Allen quickly and kindly changed the subject. He had seen part of the incident from above, he said. Apparently, the attacker was a V-gallery porter who had been sweeping the flats with a push broom. When another inmate appeared, walking down the flats, the porter attacked him, first breaking the broom handle over his head and then trying to gouge his face with the splintered ends. How the third inmate got involved, Allen didn't know.

Allen had already seen a lot of action. "You heard about the guy who hung up yesterday?" he asked me. I'd heard it mentioned at lineup, a minor news item; for seasoned officers, this was a mundane occurrence. "I was there when they cut him down," Allen told me. "He'd tied his shoelaces up high on the bars, but I guess not high enough to kill him, so he's there all pale going *gaagaagaaghh*." Allen, a natural comedian, was so funny making this sound with his eyes bugging out that I laughed despite myself. "We cut him down, then we carried him to the infirmary. My God, this place is crazy." Allen, who had previously worked in juvenile detention for the Division for Youth, knew from crazy.

He left me to my thoughts, which mainly concerned my own adequacy. There would be no official repercussions—no sergeant had seen what happened, and Orrico hadn't turned me in. But the incident troubled me. Was I up to the job, to the frequent emergencies? A couple of days before, while hustling up a staircase to back up an officer who was arguing heatedly with an inmate, I'd slipped and my baton had popped out of its ring, bouncing loudly down the metal stairs to the hands of officers below—a total embarrassment. And now this. During various crises in my prior life, I had responded well, keeping cool when a friend broke his leg skiing or when a girlfriend lacerated her leg in a fall from a motorcycle or when something in the oven caught fire. I was the guy who, when someone tripped over the cord, caught the falling lamp.

Somehow, that didn't seem to translate to prison work. I wondered about the reason. During those other incidents, my starting point was a calm, which was then interrupted. The starting point in prison, however, was stress, much of it born of hostility. Early indications were that I didn't handle it so well. . . .

Stealing Food

I worked a day in Tappan [the medium security unit of Sing Sing] with Officer St. George, who was waiting to be transferred up north. He was slow and flaccid, with the kind of world-weary negativism you might find in employees behind the counter of a fast-food restaurant at a highway rest stop. Though Tappan was a good post by most measures—relatively low-stress, relatively low-danger—he hated life at Sing Sing so much that at 3 P.M. he would hit the road to spend a single day off at home, which was six hours away, on the Canadian border. He'd take a nap the next day and then start driving again at midnight in order to make lineup at 6:45 A.M.

"What town?" I asked, and he shushed me—rightly: He didn't want inmates to know anything about him. This was the reason we didn't have our first name on our tags—only an initial—and didn't reveal other personal information. The reasons for this were best summed up by a story, possibly apocryphal, that I'd already heard at the Academy but which St. George recounted again: A CO (Correction Officer) pisses off an influential inmate in his block. Three days later, the prisoner hands him a manila envelope. Inside are photos of the CO's daughter at play on her swing set.

Most of the day, St. George sat at a desk facing the door to a stairwell and argued with inmates. He argued over whose turn it was to sweep and mop the floor. (The names were listed on a chart, so there didn't seem to be grounds for disagreement, but the inmates could see that St. George had an endless capacity to argue, and probably figured they should take advantage of it.) He argued over when the television could be on, when inmates could cook in the kitchen, and whether someone could leave a box of personal stuff in a common area. And, in the day's most interesting incident, he argued with an inmate who came in after working in the mess hall with his shirt stuffed with stolen food.

If the inmate hadn't been greedy, I thought, he might have gotten away with it. But the buttons on his shirtfront could barely contain everything he had taken: two loaves of bread, twenty-four frozen waffles, and a ten-pound bag of apples. St. George made him take it all out and put it on the desk. Leaving the mess hall with food was theft of state property, an offense right out of the book. But St. George couldn't decide what to do. Instead of writing the guy up, he proceeded to argue with him, and a dozen other inmates who gathered around, about the fate of the contraband. With the fervor of lawyers, the inmates tried to convince St. George that mess-hall workers were paid so little they *deserved* any extras they could find. ("That's a good point, you know," he told me.) One proposed that the officer simply divide the food evenly among the seventy-five inmates on the floor. "Nobody would tell," he asserted with a straight face. Yet another, tired of arguing, tried simply to intimidate St. George. "You think it's a good idea to piss off this many people with just you here, CO?" Not only did St. George fail to write this inmate up for making a threat; he later concurred with him, telling me, "You really could get a knife in your back at any time around here." Of course you could, I wanted to say, but that wasn't the point.

Seeing Inmates As Savages

Still undecided, St. George called the mess-hall officer to fill him in. The man appeared to be about as concerned over the theft as St. George was. Certainly, he didn't care about reclaiming the food. "Just write him up for 116.10 [a theft infraction]," I suggested. "That's what the training officer told us to do." St. George seemed alarmed. I think he had just remembered that the training officers debriefed the OJTs [on-the-job trainees] every day and reviewed the actions of regular officers. Suddenly he appeared to be afraid that I was going to tell our superiors about the incident. He placed all the food in a locker and told the inmates that he'd decide later what to do about it. When I got my lunch bag from the locker a while later, I saw that half the waffles were no longer there, and asked about it. "Aw, I gave them to him," St. George said. "But don't get me wrong about these guys," he added. "I wouldn't piss on 'em if they was on fire."

At 11 A.M., a blustery Neanderthal named Melman showed up on the floor to help with the count. He was annoyed because he had just come back from a drive home to discover that a pot of stew he'd put into the communal refrigerator at the Harlem Valley Psychiatric Center had been eaten. He had a bad temper, he admitted, telling how last week he had drawn his baton on an inmate in the tunnel leading up from Tappan. He couldn't wait to transfer, because, he said, "I don't want to work at a place where you tell them to step in, and they say, '*Fuck you*, CO!'" I found myself sympathetic to that idea, to the sentiment that officers deserved better than they got here.

Like our training officer, this man was fond of referring to inmates, out of their presence, as "crooks" and "mutts." The conversation left me thinking about the many reasons that an officer might come to regard inmates as savages. If a savage dissed you, what did it matter? And if a savage got hurt (particularly due to an error on your part), who cared?

The Rewarding Work of a Prison Activist

Jackie Katounas

Jackie Katounas is a restorative justice advocate and practitioner with Prison Fellowship New Zealand. Restorative justice advocates espouse four steps to repairing the damage and pain caused by criminal behavior. These steps involve giving the offender and the victims a chance to meet, allowing the offender to make amends for his or her crime, then helping the criminal reintegrate into the community. The final step is to provide the victims, the prisoners, and any other community members affected by the crime opportunities to work together to mitigate the harm caused by the crime. In this selection Katounas writes about a story of healing seven years after a terrible murder in New Zealand. The sister of a man who had been murdered wished to meet the criminal who took her brother's life. Katounas writes that at first she was wary of the woman's motivation but decided to let her meet the man who murdered her brother. Katounas states that she was surprised at the meeting when, instead of anger, the woman showed forgiveness to her brother's killer. Katounas concludes that the meeting reaffirmed her own commitment to the tenets of restorative justice.

I have never been able to fully understand the resistance to restorative justice processes within our criminal justice system. People seem to want to take ownership of a victim's hurt and trauma without considering what it is the victim needs or wants.

So often I have seen victims of crime begin a healing process that can only begin with meeting the perpetrator face to face. Victims of crime need to be heard and given an opportu-

Jackie Katounas, "A Story of Healing," *Restorative Justice Online*, August 2004. Reprinted with permission of the author.

nity to have direct dialogue with the person responsible for causing the hurt. Some victims are keen to enter into this process. Here is one example.

In 1997, a 19 year old boy killed a man. In 2004, the sister of the deceased requested an opportunity to meet face to face with this young offender. Although she lives in Australia, she had a planned trip to New Zealand and wished to explore this option whilst she was here on holiday.

Meeting with the Inmate

I first met with the inmate to assess whether a face-to-face meeting would be positive and safe for all who would enter into the process. To do so, I travelled to Wellington [New Zealand] with Rex Couper, an associate Chaplain at HB Prison, who had agreed to be my recorder during the process.

As I entered Mt Crawford Prison in Wellington, I was abruptly reminded what a dismal and bleak environment prisons are. Although I enter into many prisons throughout the country because of my work, and although it has been 10 years since I myself was incarcerated, I was shocked at my own reaction.

I remembered all too clearly how my life at that time had no hope or purpose. This intimate knowledge of what it is like to be an "inmate" reminded me of how far the Lord has brought me by his grace.

I was also surprised when this young bright-faced man entered into the room. He didn't look like a killer (he didn't have "killer" tattooed across his forehead!), and as I looked into his eyes I felt a huge sadness for the waste of life—not only his victim's but his as well.

Reflecting on Grace

I told him who I was and why I was there. A huge smile broke out across his face, and he said, "This is something that I have dreamed about for a long time." He explained that he had yearned for an opportunity to face this family. He wanted to be accountable to them for what he had done all those years ago. He wanted to say how sorry he was. I was very impressed with his positive attitude and his outlook on the future.

As we returned to Napier [New Zealand], my mind was swimming with questions:

Why does this woman want to meet him?

What could they possibly say to one another?

How would I feel in their situation?

Those questions led me to reflect on God's loving grace. I became so aware that it can only be through the grace of our Lord that such wounds can be healed.

When the time for the meeting came, I travelled again to Wellington to meet with the victim's sister (I'll call her Susan for reasons of privacy). Susan was very nervous and fearful as she looked toward this meeting, but she was also determined to do it. When I asked her why, her response astounded me.

"If he is to have any sort of future," she said, "I think meeting me might help him move on and put it behind him."

Hang on a minute, I thought. Where is this woman's anger? There was no anger or bitterness in Susan, just a huge sadness for her loss and also the offender's. Her generosity of spirit amazed me.

The Day of the Conference

On the day of the conference, it was typical Wellington weather, cold, wet and uninviting. The prison felt just like the weather, and some officers expressed scepticism about how this would work out. However, I trusted God and the process, and was quietly confident this was going to be a great conference in spite of the butterflies in my tummy.

Present at the meeting were Susan, a friend of hers who is also a counsellor, the offender, Rex, the chaplain of the prison, and myself. The conference started awkwardly as most do, but once the dialogue started it just flowed. I really didn't have to do much at all. It just happened before my eyes. It was awesome.

I won't go into details of their conversation, but at the close of the conference Susan said something very profound to the offender: "Through this tragedy you and I are connected for life. Don't let my brother's life be for nothing. I want you to get out of here and make something of your life." Then Susan hugged the man who had murdered her brother and wished him well.

Once everyone had left the room I was alone with the offender. I looked into his eyes and was prompted to put my arms around him as he sobbed his heart out. All I could do was hold him and cry, too. There were no words to say.

Miracle of Restoration

I have spoken to Susan since she has returned to Australia. She feels she can fully move on with her life now. She is glad she went through the restorative justice process.

When I witness these miracles happening is it any wonder I'm so passionate about my work? I feel privileged and honoured to be an instrument as God administers his wonderful Grace.

Some people believe that restorative justice processes are not suitable for serious crimes. My answer to that is very simple: "Come work with me for one day."

Volunteering at a Woman's Prison

Lauren Rooker

In this selection teacher and writer Lauren Rooker describes a creative writing and theater education program that she initiated as a volunteer at the Fluvanna Correctional Center for Women, Virginia's only maximum-security women's prison. She writes of the struggle to maintain the acting program with little funding, low student-retention rates, and censorship from prison officials. Despite the obstacles, Rooker persevered with her students until the completion and performance of a play written by the inmates about their life in prison. Rooker's Voice Project continues under the direction of Live Arts Upstairs Theater in Charlottesville, Virginia. Rooker now works as a middle-school teacher and freelance writer in Nashville, Tennessee.

> I don't know exactly where I escape to when I am in the class, but I am no longer encircled by the fences that close me in. I am mentally free to speak my mind, to voice my opinion without judgment or condemnation. It is truly a gift of sorts—to be able to have space within these walls— They can have me, but they can't have my mind. Hurry back. I really need this class for my peace of mind.
>
> *—excerpt from a Voice Project participant's journal*

Three months after my initial phone call to the prison and still no word. I had telephoned and e-mailed every week. I had met with the prison's program coordinator and completed volunteer training. I had taken a month off work to find funding, create a syllabus, gather materials, recruit volunteers, and meet with community members who work in offender advocacy and arts education. In a last-ditch effort, I

Lauren Rooker, "The Voice Project: Speaking Out of Necessity," *Iris: A Journal About Women*, Spring/Summer 2004, No. 48, p. 18. Copyright 2004 the Rector and visitors of the University of Virginia, on behalf of the University of Virginia Women's Center. Reproduced by permission.

had implored a state representative to contact the warden on my behalf. Now I was driving downtown—the backseat of my car overflowing with books about prison reformation, my trunk packed with photocopies, composition books, and art supplies. The generous support—professional, financial, and emotional—of countless individuals and organizations was weighing on my mind. I had no students to teach and no actual program in the present or foreseeable future. A red light brought me to a standstill; now I would be even later for my dinner shift at the restaurant, and Lord knows what hell I'd catch for it. That's when I got the call: "Can you teach at the prison next Friday?"

Two weeks before our opening performance of *Getting Out*, my college theatre troupe visited Virginia's only maximum-security women's prison. Our mission: to study the environment so that we could portray it accurately and responsibly on stage. I felt like a tourist at the zoo as I watched women behind glass walls smile and wave, flick us off, or simply carry on with their daily routines—uninterested in another face destined to leave them behind. I noted the combination of aggression and utter passivity in the inmates' body language and how the correctional officers' voices lightened when they addressed visitors. The deadening constancy of a prison environment invaded my senses: white walls, white floor, the institution-clean smell, and the maddening hum of fluorescent lights punctuated by the occasional tennis-shoe-on-linoleum screech.

In the segregation wing, an officer showed us the inmates' scant accommodations: a cinderblock room with a sink, a toilet, a platform equipped with arm and leg restraints for a bed, a metal door with a slit to receive food. No windows, no objects, no material: nothing that a woman could use to harm herself. Neither book nor blanket was permitted. The monitor station housed an arsenal—complete with riot gear, guns, ammunition, and a cattle prod—in case an inmate became violent. Our tour guide explained the necessity of such measures: segregation-housed inmates posed a threat to institutional security. Women sentenced to segregation lived in isolation as punishment for a variety of infractions, from harboring possessions that violated prison code to inciting riot to attempting escape. Despite the officer's warning that these inmates were often the most dangerous and manipulative, I had difficulty imagining what an unarmed woman kept in 24-hour lockdown could do to warrant zapping her with a cattle prod. When I inquired about this, our guide grunted a laugh and assured me that weapons were only used when absolutely necessary.

Meeting Rhonda

Outside, two women stood in the small, fenced-in area where inmates who behaved well in segregation could spend their daily fifteen minutes of recreation time. The space was barely large enough for a woman to lie down, much less exercise. The two women were trying to talk to us through the wire and glass. I stopped long enough to lip-read, "Where are you from?" I used my arms to spell out, "U.V.A." [University of Virginia] The women jumped up and down, waved their arms, and the short blonde one screamed, "Go Hood!"

By the time the last prison door clicked behind me, I knew I wanted to return—but not as I had come this time, not as a taker. Enough people had gathered what they needed from these women only to discard them. I wanted to share an exchange with them. I wanted to be a continuous presence in their lives. How I would arrange this, I had no idea. After all, I was only twenty and I still had another year of college to navigate. Nineteen months later, I would be rehearsing *Macbeth* with the small blonde from segregation.

Rhonda communicated in two ways: silence and rant. Her attendance was spotty, and when she did show, she was often late and hadn't completed her assignments. When asked, "How often do you read?" she replied, "I really don't read unless I'm locked down. I have to be bored to death to finish a book from start to finish." During her many trips to prison she had started the GED [general educational development] program three times and vocational programs twice but had completed none of them. "You know a card game will come along or I won't feel well or I'll wind up in seg," she explained.

Her writing voice—adamant and angry—benefited from the ferocious will that landed her in prison. She wrote her truth her way, and her grammar and spelling were flawless to boot. She was that rare student who could lead her peers either down the hall and out the door before I blinked or right into my hands. I wanted to harness her—not only for her own good and the success of the class but also for the sake of my ego. I wanted to be the teacher who created a structure that would nurture, challenge, and channel her impulses. I wanted to help her finish something.

After two weeks of silence, Rhonda flooded. She started by reading her free-write aloud and describing its genesis. A few minutes later she was ranting about her back-stabbing roommate, the last time she was in "seg," life on the outside, and the crazy bitch that got her sent back to lockdown. A bulldozer ground me into the dirt: until now the problem had been getting my students to talk openly. Wouldn't it be hypocritical of me to silence her? But I wasn't a therapist. I wasn't trained to deal with this. I was a poet and a teacher and this was class time. I had an obligation to the other students to maintain a balanced, safe environment. I needed to refocus her. I needed to build a dam.

"Ronda," I interrupted, "we need to establish some boundaries. Our relationships and work here are professional. I'm not interested in your personal lives and I'm not interested in your crimes. I'm interested in your creative growth. If your artistic work reveals information about your crime or your personal life, so be it; none of us should have to hide ourselves from our art or deny our experiences. But the focus of our discussion is craftsmanship, not circumstance." Silence. Then, "I got you." Despite the encouraging response, Rhonda missed more classes in the following weeks, and she finally disappeared altogether. Eventually, I learned that she was back in segregation.

Learning Crucial Survival Lessons

Before making her exit, Rhonda wised me up to two lessons crucial to my survival in the prison system and to the success of the Voice Project. I had already grown familiar with and accepted both lessons as a writer, but I had yet to consciously apply them to the art of teaching. Lesson #1: Freedom is inherently bound to form.

My seminal dream for the Voice Project was to free female inmates from literal, metaphorical, and historical prisons through art, education, and community. I never considered the difference between bars and boundaries and that the violent imposition of the former doesn't inherently mitigate the potential benefits of the latter. Inmates need both freedom and form as much as, if not more than, any other student population. Women in prison are told when to sleep, eat, and shower. They are told where to go and when and how to go there. As inmates near their release time, they worry about the choices they will encounter on the outside. Too much freedom often creates panic, and panic rarely fosters articulate expression. The more specifically I articulated expectations and guidelines, the more fluently, freely, and deeply they worked.

However, I refused to belittle grown women by addressing them like schoolchildren, and I never wanted our community boundaries to resemble the daily commands that sounded over the prison's loudspeaker. To avoid this, I tried to create opportunities for the students to have agency whenever possible, and we always discussed why we were doing a particular exercise, even if the decision to do it had been entirely mine.

If an individual disagreed with my reasoning, at least she possessed an engaged understanding of my purposes and could respond to the process as an informed participant.

Facing Prison's Stark Realities

Learning to create a balanced classroom environment proved less difficult than maintaining my own professional and psychological freedom. There were days when, despite my love for my students and the work we shared, I couldn't race through security clearance and out to my car fast enough. As a volunteer, I could comply with the prison administration or I could leave. Prison staff regularly entered my classroom unannounced. On multiple occasions correctional officers interrupted my class to remove students without explanation. Sometimes the women returned and sometimes they didn't. Our classroom space, supplies, meeting time, and student roster were subject to change without advance notice. The realities of prison often left my students and me feeling violated. Only by working through these challenges did we learn how to cultivate closeness and trust in an ever-changing community, how to create art only from the necessary, and, quite painfully, how to continue creating in the face of group loss and lack of artistic autonomy.

Rhonda's second lesson: I would fail. I started the Voice Project assuming it would succeed. Of course, I knew there was the possibility of failure and, at times, reason told me that such an outcome was probable. However, I couldn't secure funding and volunteers, much less the commitment and trust of the prison administration and my students, if I didn't show unflinching belief in the project. What I had not fully anticipated was how many ways I would want to help my students and, consequently, how many ways I could fail them.

When I arrived at the prison to teach my first class I knew some facts about women incarcerated in the United States: 40–50 percent of them are survivors of abuse; 25 percent of them are physically or sexually abused before the age of eighteen; 75 percent are mothers; female inmates' children are five to six times more likely to be incarcerated than their peers; education and medical care for inmates is suffering due to budget cuts and the currently popular political ideology that prisons are for punishment, not rehabilitation. Yet I did not—could not—have prepared for the guilt and powerlessness I felt when I encountered the living proof of these facts in the faces that looked to me for guidance. I took comfort in the fact that although our country's ailing correctional system and its mistreatment of women affected my work at the prison, in my role as an artist and teacher, the larger system's failures were not my individual responsibility. Still, the hard realities of my students' lives pressed upon my conscience.

I experienced more difficulty coping with disappointments directly related to the Voice Project—most notably a low student retention rate and censorship—than with larger institutional woes, perhaps because I had anticipated possessing a certain level of autonomy within my own program. During eight months at the prison, I worked with thirteen women. Only five completed the program. Five stopped attending out of choice, and three were sent to segregation, thereby losing all privileges—including education. One participant went to segregation only four days shy of our final performance. Once a woman was in segregation, I could have no contact with her. I couldn't even return her journal to her.

I used to wonder how I could have served these women better, whether circumstances would be different if I had inspired them more deeply or offered them more support. The encouragement of friends who constantly reminded me that offering inmates anything was better than nothing failed to comfort me. How could I establish a safe haven in which to create if I couldn't prevent correctional officers from entering our classroom and hauling my students away? How could I encourage openness and honesty in my students' writing if their journals could be confiscated by prison authorities? How could I be a consistent, reliable presence in these women's lives if my class could be cancelled without consulting me?

I Became the Student

Now, humbled by my experiences and by my students' resilient spirits, I understand both the smallness and the effectiveness of the Voice Project. I'm thinking of Jordan. The night before the women of the Voice Project were scheduled to perform their original play for an audience of inmates, prison staff, and program supporters, the prison administration mandated that a significant portion of my students' work be cut from the program due to "inappropriate content." (Poems about romantic love, sexual abuse, and homosexuality were all deemed "inappropriate." This incident is representative of the correctional system's denial of the significant roles gender and sexuality play in shaping the identity of female inmates.) On the morning of our performance, I met with my students to tell them about the administration's decision and to rehearse our newly abbreviated script. Jordan, thin from a recent bout of pneumonia and wheelchair-bound with a broken foot, openly wept as I informed the group that two of her three monologues had been cut. I went on to identify the other censored scenes and explain that in order to ensure the Voice Project's continuance we had only one choice: to perform the censored version of our script. When I finished Jordan stared up at me and said, "We'll do it."

That day my students did not perform the play they had intended, the play they had spent months tirelessly writing, revising, and rehearsing. They were not permitted to speak from the fullness of their hearts, minds, bodies, and experiences. But they were not silenced. They raised their voices—perhaps even more courageously in light of the censorship to which they were subjected. They gave of themselves generously and, in doing so, I hope they inspired and challenged their audience members, whether incarcerated or not, to do the same.

I started the Voice Project with the hope of creating a community of trust where my imprisoned sisters—women who are too often silenced politically, economically, socially, emotionally, and physically—could experience the joy, challenges, passion and power of soulful, creative expression. During the process, I hoped to impart practical skills to the inmates and forge a more intimate relationship between my state's artistic community and the women incarcerated in our maximum security prison. However, when I began the program I didn't anticipate that my students would teach me about the vital necessities of creation and community. Sometimes we create to amuse, heal, practice, honor, remember, or pass the time. Sometimes we create to survive—a truth that we can, perhaps, forget more easily when our lives are comfortable. But rob us of our family, friends, home, health, education, security, and the basic freedom to speak and move as we desire, and what will we have? Strip away all that we cling to and cherish and what will we do? Take all but our minds, bodies, voices, and a battered hope in humanity and what will we make? How will we live and what will we give? In the words of a Voice Project participant who is serving life in prison, "I arrest my pen and sentence it to paper."

SOCIAL ISSUES
FIRSTHAND

CHAPTER 3

Prisoners' Family Members

Mother's Day in Prison

Amanda Coyne

*In this selection Amanda Coyne provides a personal account of
visiting her sister in federal prison camp on Mother's Day. She
also describes the other female inmates in the visiting room, including Stephanie, whose young son was visiting. While Coyne's
nephew was happy and hopeful despite his mother's imprisonment, Stephanie's son was bitter and resentful. Coyne writes that
she, her other sister, and her brother strive to help their nephew
maintain a positive attitude during his mother's incarceration by
showering him with love and attention. She worries, however,
that her sister's imprisonment will have a lasting, negative impact on her nephew. Amanda Coyne is a freelance writer living
in Anchorage, Alaska. Her articles have appeared in the* New
York Times Magazine *and* Bust Magazine *and have been read
on the Alaskan Public Radio and the National Public Radio net-
works.*

You can spot the convict-moms here in the visiting room
by the way they hold and touch their children and by the
single flower that is perched in front of them—a rose, a tulip,
a daffodil. Many of these mothers have untied the bow that
attaches the flower to its silver-and-red cellophane wrapper
and are using one of the many empty soda cans at hand as a
vase. They sit proudly before their flower-in-a-Coke-can, amid
Hershey bar wrappers, half-eaten Ding Dongs, and empty paper coffee cups. Occasionally, a mother will pick up her present
and bring it to her nose when one of the bearers of the single
flower—her child—asks if she likes it. And the mother will respond the way that mothers always have and always will respond when presented with a gift on this day. "Oh, I just love

it. It's perfect, I'll put it in the middle of my Bible." Or, "I'll put it on my desk, right next to your school picture." And always: "It's the best one here."

But most of what is being smelled today is the children themselves. While the other adults are plunking coins into the vending machines, the mothers take deep whiffs from the backs of their children's necks, or kiss and smell the backs of their knees, or take off their shoes and tickle their feet and then pull them close to their noses. They hold them tight and take in their own second scent—the scent assuring them that these are still their children and that they still belong to them.

The visitors are allowed to bring in pockets full of coins, and today that Mother's Day flower, and I know from previous visits to my older sister here at the Federal Prison Camp for women in Pekin, Illinois, that there is always an aberrant urge to gather immediately around the vending machines. The sandwiches are stale, the coffee weak, the candy bars the ones we always pass up in a convenience store. But after we hand the children over to their mothers, we gravitate toward those machines. Like milling in the kitchen at a party. We all do it, and nobody knows why. Polite conversation ensues around the microwave while the popcorn is popping and the processed-chicken sandwiches are being heated. We ask one another where we are from, how long a drive we had. An occasional whistle through the teeth, a shake of the head. "My, my, long way from home, huh?" "Staying at the Super 8 right up the road. Not a bad place." "Stayed at the Econo Lodge last time. Wasn't a good place at all." Never asking the questions we really want to ask: "What's she in for?" "How much time's she got left?" You never ask in the waiting room of a doctor's office either. Eventually, all of us—fathers, mothers, sisters, brothers, a few boyfriends, and very few husbands—return to the queen of the day, sitting at a fold-out table loaded with snacks, prepared for five or so hours of attempted normal conversation.

Dressed in Their Sunday-Best

Most of the inmates are elaborately dressed, many in prison-crafted dresses and sweaters in bright blues and pinks. They wear meticulously applied makeup in corresponding hues, and their hair is replete with loops and curls—hair that only women with the time have the time for. Some of the better seamstresses have crocheted vests and purses to match their outfits. Although the world outside would never accuse these women of making haute-couture fashion statements, the fathers and the sons and the boyfriends and the very few husbands think they look beautiful, and they tell them so repeatedly. And I can imagine the hours spent preparing for this visit—hours of needles and hooks clicking over brightly colored yards of yarn. The hours of discussing, dissecting, and bragging about these visitors—especially the men. Hours spent in the other world behind the door where we're not allowed, sharing lipsticks and mascaras, and unraveling the occasional hair-tangled hot roller, and the brushing out and lifting and teasing . . . and the giggles that abruptly change into tears without warning—things that define any female-only world. Even, or especially, if that world is a female federal prison camp.

While my sister Jennifer is with her son in the playroom, an inmate's mother comes over to introduce herself to my younger sister, Charity, my brother, John, and me. She tells us about visiting her daughter in a higher-security prison before she was transferred here. The woman looks old and tired, and her shoulders sag under the weight of her recently acquired bitterness.

"Pit of fire," she says, shaking her head. "Like a pit of fire straight from hell. Never seen anything like it. Like something out of an old movie about prisons." Her voice is getting louder and she looks at each of us with pleading eyes. "My daughter was there. Don't even get me started on that place. Women die there."

John and Charity and I silently exchange glances.

"My daughter would come to the visiting room with a black eye and I'd think, 'All she did was sit in the car while her boyfriend ran into the house.' She didn't even touch the stuff. Never even handled it."

Ten Years for Waiting in a Car

She continues to stare at us, each in turn. "Ten years. That boyfriend talked and he got three years. She didn't know anything. Had nothing to tell them. They gave her ten years. They called it conspiracy. Conspiracy? Aren't there real criminals out there?" She asks this with hands outstretched, waiting for an answer that none of us can give her.

The woman's daughter, the conspirator, is chasing her son through the maze of chairs and tables and through the other children. She's a twenty-four-year-old blonde, whom I'll call Stephanie, with Dorothy Hamill hair and matching dimples. She looks like any girl you might see in any shopping mall in middle America. She catches her chocolate-brown son and tickles him, and they laugh and trip and fall together onto the floor and laugh harder.

Had it not been for that wait in the car, this scene would be taking place at home, in a duplex Stephanie would rent while trying to finish her two-year degree in dental hygiene or respiratory therapy at the local community college. The duplex would be spotless, with a blown-up picture of her and her son over the couch and ceramic unicorns and horses occupying the shelves of the entertainment center. She would make sure that her son went to school every day with stylishly floppy pants, scrubbed teeth, and a good breakfast in his belly. Because of their difference in skin color, there would be occasional tension—caused by the strange looks from strangers, teachers, other mothers, and the bullies on the playground, who would chant after they knocked him down, "Your Momma's white, your Momma's white." But if she were home,

Before seeing her mother on Mother's Day, Briana Stevens (left) checks in with prison guards at the California Institute for Women in California, 2006. © Tim Rue/Corbis

their weekends and evenings would be spent together transcending those looks and healing those bruises. Now, however, their time is spent eating visiting-room junk food and his school days are spent fighting the boys in the playground who chant, "Your Momma's in prison, your Momma's in prison."

"Is My Mommy a Bad Guy?"

He will be ten when his mother is released, the same age my nephew will be when his mother is let out. But Jennifer, my sister, was able to spend the first five years of Toby's life with him. Stephanie had Ellie after she was incarcerated. They let her hold him for eighteen hours, then sent her back to prison. She has done the "tour," and her son is a well-traveled six-year-old. He has spent weekends visiting his mother in prisons in Kentucky, Texas, Connecticut (the Pit of Fire), and now at last here, the camp—minimum security, Pekin, Illinois.

Ellie looks older than his age. But his shoulders do not droop like his grandmother's. On the contrary, his bitterness lifts them and his chin higher than a child's should be, and the childlike, wide-eyed curiosity has been replaced by defiance. You can see his emerging hostility as he and his mother play together. She tells him to pick up the toy that he threw, say, or to put the deck of cards away. His face turns sullen, but she persists. She takes him by the shoulders and looks him in the eye, and he uses one of his hands to swat at her. She grabs the hand and he swats with the other. Eventually, she pulls him toward her and smells the top of his head, and she picks up the cards or the toy herself. After all, it is Mother's Day and she sees him so rarely. But her acquiescence makes him angrier, and he stalks out of the playroom with his shoulders thrown back.

Toby, my brother and sister and I assure one another, will not have these resentments. He is better taken care of than most. He is living with relatives in Wisconsin. Good, solid, middle-class, churchgoing relatives. And when he visits us, his aunts and his uncle, we take him out for adventures where we walk down the alley of a city and pretend that we are being chased by the "bad guys." We buy him fast food, and his uncle, John, keeps him up well past his bedtime enthralling him with stories of the monkeys he met in India. A perfect mix, we try to convince one another. Until we take him to see his mother and on the drive back he asks the question that most confuses him, and no doubt all the other children who spend much of their lives in prison visiting rooms: "Is my Mommy a bad guy?" It is the question that most seriously disorders his five-year-old need to clearly separate right from wrong. And because our own need is perhaps just as great, it is the question that haunts us as well.

The Answer Isn't That Simple

Now, however, the answer is relatively simple. In a few years, it won't be. In a few years we will have to explain mandatory minimums, and the war on drugs, and the murky conspiracy laws, and the enormous amount of money and time that federal agents pump into imprisoning low-level drug dealers and those who happen to be their friends and their lovers. In a few years he might have the reasoning skills to ask why so many armed robbers and rapists and child-molesters and, indeed, murderers are punished less severely than his mother. When he is older, we will somehow have to explain to him the difference between federal crimes which don't allow for parole, and state crimes, which do. We will have to explain that his mother was taken from him for five years not because she was a drug dealer but because she made four phone calls for someone she loved.

But we also know it is vitally important that we explain all this without betraying our bitterness. We understand the danger of abstract anger, of being disillusioned with your country, and, most of all, we do not want him to inherit that legacy. We would still like him to be raised as we were, with the idea that we live in the best country in the world with the best legal system in the world—a legal system carefully designed to be immune to political mood swings and public hysteria; a system that promises to fit the punishment to the crime. We want him to be a good citizen. We want him to have absolute faith that he lives in a fair country, a country that watches over and protects its most vulnerable citizens: its women and children.

So for now we simply say, "Toby, your mother isn't bad, she just did a bad thing. Like when you put rocks in the lawn mower's gas tank. You weren't bad then, you just did a bad thing."

Once, after being given this weak explanation, he said, "I wish I could have done something really bad, like my Mommy. So I could go to prison too and be with her." . . .

Rebelling Against the System

Back at our table; . . . Charity resumes her conversation with a nineteen-year-old ex–New York University student—another conspirator. Eight years.

Prison, it seems, has done little to squelch the teenager's rebellious nature. She has recently been released from solitary confinement. She wears new retro-bellbottom jeans and black shoes with big clunky heels. Her hair is short, clipped perfectly ragged and dyed white—all except the roots, which are a stylish black. She has beautiful pale skin and beautiful red lips. She looks like any midwestern coed trying to escape her origins by claiming New York's East Village as home. She steals the bleach from the laundry room, I learn later, in order to maintain that fashionable white hue. But stealing the bleach is not what landed her in the hole [solitary confinement]. She committed the inexcusable act of defacing federal property. She took one of her government-issue T-shirts and wrote in permanent black magic marker, "I have been in your system. I have examined your system." And when she turned around it read, "I find it very much in need of repair."

But Charity has more important things to discuss with the girl than rebelling against the system. They are talking fashion. They talk prints versus plains, spring shoes, and spring dresses. Charity informs the girl that sling-back, high-heeled sandals and pastels are all the rage. She makes a disgusted face and says, "Damn! Pinks and blues wash me out. I hate pastels. I don't have any pastels."

This fashion blip seems to be putting the girl into a deep depression. And so Charity, attempting to lighten up the conversation, puts her nose toward the girl's neck.

"New Armani scent, Gio," my sister announces.

The girl perks up. She nods her head. She calls one of the other inmates over.

Charity performs the same ritual: "Coco Chanel." And again: "Paris, Yves St. Laurent."

The line gets longer, and the girls talk excitedly to one another. It seems that Charity's uncanny talent for divining brand-name perfumes is perhaps nowhere on earth more appreciated than here with these sensory-starved inmates. . . .

"Obsession. Calvin Klein," I hear my sister pronounce. The girls cheer in unison. . . .

The Visit Ends

It's now 3:00. Visiting ends at 3:30. The kids are getting cranky, and the adults are both exhausted and wired from too many hours of conversation, too much coffee and candy. The fathers, mothers, sisters, brothers, and the few boyfriends, and the very few husbands are beginning to show signs of gathering the trash. The mothers of the infants are giving their heads one last whiff before tucking them and their paraphernalia into their respective carrying cases. The visitors meander toward the door, leaving the older children with their mothers for one last word. But the mothers never say what they want to say to their children. They say things like, "Do well in school," "Be nice to your sister," "Be good for Aunt Betty, or Grandma." They don't say, "I'm sorry I'm sorry I'm sorry. I love you more than anything else in the world and I think about you every minute and I worry about you with a pain that shoots straight to my heart, a pain so great I think I will just burst when I think of you alone, without me. I'm sorry."

We are standing in front of the double glass doors that lead to the outside world. My older sister holds her son, rocking him gently. They are both crying. We give her a look and she puts him down. Charity and I grasp each of his small hands, and the four of us walk through the doors. As we're walking out, my brother sings one of his banana songs to Toby.

"Take me out to the—" and Toby yells out, "Banana store!"

"Buy me some—"

"Bananas!!"

"I don't care if I ever come back. For it's root, root, root for the—"

"Monkey team!"

I turn back and see a line of women standing behind the glass wall. Some of them are crying, but many simply stare with dazed eyes. Stephanie is holding both of her son's hands in hers and speaking urgently to him. He is struggling, and his head is twisting violently back and forth. He frees one of his hands from her grasp, balls up his fist, and punches her in the face. Then he walks with purpose through the glass doors and out the exit. I look back at her. She is still in a crouched position. She stares, unblinking, through those doors. Her hands have left her face and are hanging on either side of her. I look away, but before I do, I see drops of blood drip from her nose, down her chin, and onto the shiny marble floor.

Coping with a Father in Prison

Ronnie O'Sullivan, interviewed by Lucy Keenan

In this interview written by Lucy Keenan with the Action for Prisoners' Families organization based in London, British snooker (a game similar to pool) ace Ronnie O'Sullivan reveals the horror and shock he felt as a young boy when his dad was sentenced to life in prison for murder. In the interview O'Sullivan describes how he was treated by classmates at school and his first visit to his dad in prison. He states that British prison officials make it tough for families to visit their loved ones in prison. Because of the barriers that prisoners' families face, in 2003 the snooker star began to support the Action for Prisoners' Families organization's campaign to start a national, free telephone help line for prisoners' families in London. The help line is a free and confidential service for anyone affected by the imprisonment of a close family member or friend. Counselors with the help line provide families with information and guidance about prisons in England and Wales. They also help link the families with different services and local support groups in their areas. O'Sullivan also advocates more visiting days for the families of prisoners as well as the building of visiting centers in prison that include playground facilities for children.

O'Sullivan has also written an autobiography entitled Ronnie.

[Keenan:] *What do you think could be done to make family ties between prisoners and families better?*

[O'Sullivan:] Let the prisoners out, back to their families!

I think sometimes having people close to home is good. The distance thing is a big thing. It can be a day out some-

Ronnie O'Sullivan, interviewed by Lucy Keenan, "Snooker Ace, Ronnie O'Sullivan Talks About His Dad's Imprisonment," *Action for Prisoners' Families News*, Autumn 2003, pp. 22–23. Reproduced by permission.

times. It can be quite expensive. In general they are trying to make it hard for you to make visits nowadays. They are trying to make it as difficult as possible. Yeah, I suppose they could make it more easier.

You have travelled England and Wales to visit the prisons your Dad's been in. How many prisons do you think your Dad has been in?

Probably about 8 or 9. I don't look at it as a chore though. I always look at it like they can put any sort of a barrier up towards me and I am still going to make every effort . . . but I can understand what you are saying. I would travel to the end of the world just for five minutes with him, but that is me.

Reaction to Imprisonment

What was your first reaction when your Dad told you he was going to prison?

Shock and horror and just sadness and gutted really. I just cried for a long time. I was just in bits.

Where did you get information about what was happening?

I just found out from my Mum really. I was too young at the time. I was just 15. My Mum was relaying what was going on to me, what was happening, where he'd be, where we could go and visit him.

I remember it being quite difficult, you know, because once he was found guilty everyone was in a state of shock. My Mum was in a state of shock. We had to find out where he was, where he would go, when we could see him, when we could talk to him. If he was all right. We just wanted to hear his voice. We didn't know what to do. It was only because of people with experience who already knew what to do, that sort of thing. I think it is a lot different now. Oh . . . I'm not so sure if it is different.

What about you and your sister? What kind of reactions did you get from friends and at school?

Yeah, I think there were a few things that were said—you could take it personal. I got things that were said to me that wasn't very nice, but you know, it didn't bother me at the time. It did, . . . but I wouldn't show weakness to anybody. There was a bit of a stigma and people judge you without knowing you really. They think your Dad is a murderer so you must like violence and it couldn't be further from the truth. A lot of people say to me that you are not what I expected you to be when they actually meet me, so it does become that sort of thing when people judge you without really knowing you because of your background and family sometimes.

The First Visit

What was your first visit like?

I remember my first visit very clearly. It was just me and my Mum. My Mum used to go up there every day when he was on remand and I remember going to see him for the first time and it was horrible, really horrible.

Did you see him in a room with lots of other people as well?

Yeah, it was Brixton and it was a big long queue [line] and he was on one side and we was on the other. There was a barrier thing that separated you from the inmate.

If you could change one thing about the way you visit what would it be?

I would definitely like more days where you've got longer with the person. Maybe not stuck in a room, maybe you could go out. I wouldn't mind going into the prison, sitting in the grounds having a picnic.

Some prisons do all-day visits. Would you like all-day visits and things like that at Christmas?

Sometimes I have been able to go in the morning and the afternoon, a double visit, and they are quite good, but sometimes it would be really nice to be outside, you know, because all you're doing, . . . is stuck in a room; it can be quite claustrophobic. You just want to have a laugh you know, sometimes in the visits room it can be quite depressing.

Sticking Together As a Family

What do you think generally about the facilities for kids in the visitors' centres?

Not the best, some prisons are better than others. I have been to prisons where they have play areas for kids and it keeps them quite quiet, but sometimes you can go on a visit and the kids get bored and they start screaming and shouting. Yeah, it could be better. They [the prisons] haven't got a lot of money though.

You talk about your father a great deal in your book and it is obvious that you are very close and he has been very supportive. How did you manage to maintain the family unit while he has been inside?

I think he has been stronger than me and my sister, all the way through it, and possibly my Mum. He is the strongest one out of the family and if anything he is the reason why I am what I am today, because if I had someone who had broken down in prison that would have been a great excuse for me to think, if he has done it, I am going do it. But he kept himself together. We all sort of push each other on. If he is not too great I try and gee [cheer] him up. It's like the weakest link—we try and keep everyone strong because if one person isn't, it can make the whole lot fall apart and we don't want that to happen. It's about being there for each other and it's not easy.

Reflections by a Son of Two Inmates

Chesa Boudin

When Chesa Boudin was fourteen months old, his parents com-mitted armed robbery and murder and were sentenced to more than seventy-five years in prison. Boudin was then adopted by another couple. While visiting his birth mother in prison, he met Lorenzo, whose mother had been sentenced to the same prison because of drug-related crimes. They grew up meeting each other on visiting days, but their lives took very different paths. Lorenzo was sent to prison while Boudin went to Yale. In this excerpt Boudin writes about what he feels are the reasons for the differ-ent paths that the two men took. One reason, he says, is social and economic differences in their backgrounds. Boudin is from an upper-class white neighborhood and attended a private school, while Lorenzo, who is black, lived in the inner city with his grandmother. Boudin writes, however, that while he believes Lorenzo is in prison because he was disadvantaged, Lorenzo himself believes his imprisonment is the result of his bad choices in life. Boudin writes, however, that Lorenzo believes he will be able to avoid being reincarcerated once he is released from prison. Boudin is a 2003 Rhodes Scholar and coauthor of The Venezu-elan Revolution: 100 Questions and 100 Answers *and coeditor of* Letters from Young Activists: Today's Rebels Speak Out. *His work has also appeared in the online magazine* Salon.com *and in the* Chicago Tribune Book Review.

"Let's play me and you against our moms," Lorenzo yelled across the patio. It was the beginning of another summer in Bedford Hills New York, just an hour's drive north of Man-hattan along the Saw Mill River Parkway. It must have been

Chesa Boudin, "From Jail to Yale," *Women and Prison: A Site for Resistance*, 2006. Re-produced by permission of the publisher and the author.

the twelfth volleyball game of the day and we had already played with every possible combination of teams. I too preferred to play with Lorenzo against our mothers. We always won, but it required teamwork and all our attention. After the exhausting volleyball game, we had a water fight, the object of which was to become as soaked as possible. Finally, we retreated inside to the cool of the air conditioning for lunch. It was our favorite day of the week—Wednesday—when our mothers ate McDonald's with us.

Lorenzo and I had become friends over the years even though he was three years older than I and we attended different schools. Those summers provided an abundance of potential playmates, but Lorenzo was my favorite; we had a special bond. I looked up to him, and he let me tag along.

After that summer Lorenzo and I lost touch. Our moms remained friends, but I guess he was growing up and so we went our separate ways. I didn't hear any news about him for a couple of years, but then my mom told me he'd won an essay writing contest. The prize was a meeting with the governor of New York and a trip to Egypt. He was excelling in the sixth grade, and I was still struggling to read. Our whole community in Bedford was so proud of him. Knowing that he would see the pyramids made me envious.

Our Bedford Hills is not the privileged Westchester County community filled with the estates of New York City's elite refugees. My Bedford, Lorenzo's Bedford, is the women's maximum-security prison located on the edge of town. Prisons became an intricate part of our childhood; as children with incarcerated parents, our chances of becoming incarcerated ourselves increase six-fold.

After a hiatus of more than a decade, I saw Lorenzo on a windy Thursday morning in October of 1999. I eagerly anticipated our meeting—what would he be like? How much would we have in common? We had exchanged a few letters arranging to meet, and all of a sudden he was walking toward me.

Wearing green pants and a red polo shirt, he looked nothing like I remembered. His hair was in cornrows and his tall, strong body complemented his good looks. Our eyes met for a moment, but I felt self-conscious and looked away. Finally we said hey and exchanged an awkward hug—hindered further by the wide table separating us. Our journeys had left us in radically different positions: he was incarcerated at Great Meadows Correctional Facility, and I was at Yale University. I was preparing for my first year at Yale when I heard that my father had met Lorenzo; they were incarcerated in the same upstate New York maximum-security prison. I know a lot of brilliant, kind people in prison, but my childhood friendship with Lorenzo and the intersections of our lives puzzled me. Why was he in prison while I was in my freshman year at Yale?

The Forgotten Victims

It was exciting to see Lorenzo and my father. We huddled at one end of the long table that runs the length of the Great Meadows visiting room. Lorenzo and my dad were on the prisoners' side, and Jeff, a friend who had driven me, and I occupied the visitors' side. I was there primarily to talk with Lorenzo, but it had been several months since I had last seen my dad, so all four of us chatted for awhile about college life and my challenge at college of balancing academics with Varsity crew. Eventually Lorenzo and I broke off into a private conversation. I wanted to hear his perspective on the different courses our lives had run.

I came with a simple, straightforward view: Lorenzo's childhood and his mother's incarceration must have led him to prison. He disagreed. "I was stupid," he said. According to Lorenzo, his incarceration was his fault; he had no excuses. Before long we were having a typical nature versus nurture argument. We could have been in a Yale dorm room. The odd thing was the sides we had chosen to argue. According to society's standards, I had achieved a measure of conventional success. Yet I attributed that primarily to my support and surroundings. Lorenzo on the other hand, was not an actively productive member of society yet was demanding responsibility for his life. He claimed that he had enjoyed all the advantages necessary, but that he had made different choices. Contextualizing our experiences as children of incarcerated parents, Lorenzo and I agreed that we are by no means anomalies.

It turns out that nationally, according to conservative estimates, there are 1.9 million children with parents in prison. The numbers are far greater if all the children who have had a parent incarcerated at some point during childhood are included. We are the unseen, forgotten victims of America's war on crime. Our numbers have dramatically increased over the past decade as the nation's race to incarcerate has led to the imprisonment of more and more parents.

When my mother and my father were sentenced to 20 years to life, and 75 years to life, respectively on robbery and felony murder charges, so was I. Lorenzo's mother, along with 68 percent of incarcerated women, is serving time for a nonviolent crime. Her offense was drug related, as are those of one third of incarcerated women. When she was sentenced to a staggering 17 years to life under New York State's Rockefeller drug laws, so were Lorenzo and his younger sister. The majority of prisoners in this country are parents with more than one child.

Growth of the Prison Industry

Since our mothers' incarcerations, the number of women in prisons has climbed faster than any other group, although men still account for 94 percent of the United States' prison population. The number of female inmates has grown at an annual rate of almost 9 percent for the last decade: an increase of 573 percent since 1981, the year my parents were arrested. The rate of incarceration for men has increased by 7 percent annually. These numbers are competitive with stock market returns even during the unprecedented boom of the 1990s. Given the extraordinary growth in the prison industry, perhaps it should come as no surprise that we now have several private prison companies with stocks traded on Wall Street.

Like our mothers, nearly 80 percent of women in prison have kids, with an average of 2.4 children each. Lorenzo, who has no children of his own, is in the minority since 55 percent of men in prison are fathers, each with an average of 2 children. What happens to all these kids?

Lorenzo, determined to convince me that if anything he had had an easier life, asked me how old I was when my parents were arrested, and how hard the separation had been for me. I was fourteen months old. I suffered from early developmental problems and told Lorenzo that as a child I was diagnosed with learning disabilities and petit mal, a form of epilepsy. I got into trouble at school and had a violent temper, as do 69.9 percent of children with incarcerated parents. Lorenzo, who was already nine when his mother was arrested, was able to stay with his grandmother and maintain contact with his father, who was never incarcerated. He held that my separation from both my parents at such a young age represented a larger obstacle than his mother's incarceration did for him.

Knowing that only 1 out of 11 children of incarcerated parents remain with a primary caregiver, I was surprised to hear that Lorenzo, like me, made only one switch. He moved from his parents to his paternal grandmother, and I went from my parents to friends of theirs who already had two sons, my instant brothers. Although neither Lorenzo nor I claimed an advantage in this regard, there is actually a direct correlation between the number of times a child changes primary caregivers and the problems he or she suffers in school. With only one change, nearly 20 percent of kids have problems in school; two changes raise the percentage to 30, and suffering three or more changes increases the percentage to 50.

Differing Socioeconomic Backgrounds

Despite the fact that we both had relatively stable family lives, I was fairly certain that he hadn't had the same opportunities as I to maintain contact with his mother. In fact, less than 50 percent of children ever visit their incarcerated mothers. Lorenzo told me that he and his sister had lived with their paternal grandmother because their maternal grandparents were so angry with their daughter that they refused to allow any contact. He admitted that he had not visited his mother regularly since our summers together, but maintained that he had a strong relationship with her nonetheless. Anyway, Lorenzo countered, unlike me and most children of incarcerated parents, he lived just an hour away from his mother. Some studies indicate that over 60 percent of such children live more than 100 miles away from their parents' prison. This challenge is particularly large for the 10 percent of children whose families lack the resources to keep them out of foster care. Although Lorenzo and I both come from families with adequate resources to keep custody, our families and our socioeconomic backgrounds differ.

Financial resources played a significant role in my development. Even at age seven, when my adoptive family moved to Chicago, we had enough money for my flights to New York to visit my parents. I was in touch with my parents throughout my childhood, seeing them almost monthly and through frequent letters and phone calls. Once I arrived in New York, I relied on numerous friends of my parents for places to stay and rides to prisons. I never had to worry about the long distance collect calls from their correctional facilities. . . .

I saw child psychiatrists from kindergarten until I was in the fourth grade. Most children are not able to verbalize their problems so therapists use what is called "play therapy" to help kids express their feelings. My first day at the psychiatrist, I wobbled in and started playing with the blocks. After I had completed my structure, the doctor asked me what I had built. "This is a prison," I said. Then pointing to two figures in the structure, I continued, "those are my parents in jail," and directing his attention to the two dolls outside my structure I told him, "those are the parents I live with."

Supportive Family Structure

For some reason I have always been unusually comfortable talking about my parents in jail. When I was younger it was often one of the first things I would tell new acquaintances. Unlike me, the other children I know with incarcerated parents are guarded about their family lives. For me, overcoming the problems connected to my separation from my parents was a long, expensive process that required a massive support network. My stable family life, as I told Lorenzo, enabled me to overcome challenges. I would not have been accepted to the University of Chicago Laboratory School in Chicago, where I had spent the previous twelve years studying, without my adoptive family's adamant support in the face of a hostile admissions board. Once accepted, I would not have been able to keep up academically without the years of heroic teachers and private tutoring. And, I would likely have been thrown out for all of my disciplinary problems, which included fighting and throwing chairs at teachers, were it not for the support of my psychiatrist and adoptive family. I argued that it was emotional and financial support that afforded me the luxury of attending my high school, boosting my chances of acceptance at a school like Yale. . . .

Lorenzo was quick to correct any potential stereotype I might have imagined about his childhood. Growing up he had not faced the same academic or social challenges as I had, and he too lived in a loving environment. Lorenzo told me that he

105

had "always had enough." His writing had won him statewide recognition and his grandmother made sure he studied hard. The work and discipline paid off and Lorenzo excelled academically, athletically, and socially. . . . Lorenzo was so successful that a family in Bedford Hills that had known him during our summers there made him a generous offer.

The Bedford family was so taken with his charisma, kindness and intelligence that they were willing to let him live with them (just a few minutes away from his mother) and have him attend a wealthy Westchester county school instead of his inner city school. Or, if he would prefer, they were willing to help him gain admission to a prep school for which they agreed to pay tuition. It was his decision. He could to go off to boarding school, move in with them, or stay with his grandmother.

Feelings of Personal Responsibility

Lorenzo's decision to stay in Brooklyn with his grandmother and sister is understandable. They are his family, and he had been with them his whole life. As much as he appreciated the offer, he felt more comfortable in Brooklyn. What would he tell all the new kids? It had been hard enough in Brooklyn, and Lorenzo never liked to talk about his mom in prison. After a while he had gotten tired of hiding it, and now enough people knew that he no longer had to explain. He didn't want to start over.

Despite my own willingness to discuss my family situation with complete strangers, I could identify with Lorenzo's discomfort. There is a certain stigma or sense of guilt associated with having incarcerated parents. At age four, after speaking on the phone to my mother, I began crying. I repeated, over and over again, "If only I could have talked; if only I could have told them not to go." Obviously I was not able to talk at fourteen months, let alone convince my parents not to get involved in a robbery. Nevertheless, only a few years later I felt at least partly responsible: I should have been able to stop them. It is natural for a child to assume that if his parents really loved him, they wouldn't have risked losing him. Lorenzo felt it too.

To this day, he also says he "feels responsible" for his incarcerated mother, and that he "needs to take care of her." When he was younger, he cared for and respected her by not talking about her outside of the family. To talk about her meant referring to her as a convict or a criminal, disrespectful to her and potentially humiliating for him. Lorenzo remembers going to school events on several occasions and having his grandmother come along. All his friends who had brought their mothers wanted to know why they never met his mom. . . .

Lorenzo had developed separate groups of friends: one at his public school, and the other in his neighborhood in Brooklyn. Gradually he began to feel more comfortable with his friends from the neighborhood. It was easier to see them; he didn't have to take the bus across town the way he did to meet up with his friends from school. All he had to do was look out the window. He started running with a group of guys who never asked about where his mother was; they didn't have mothers in the picture either. They had fierce loyalty to each other and to their neighborhood. Lorenzo had always been able to prove himself in school; eventually he felt that he had to prove himself on the streets as well. One time he took it too far.

Poor Choices

When Lorenzo was sixteen, he and his friends were riding their bikes, and before any of them knew what was going on, they were confronting a stranger on the street. A fight ensued and when it was over the stranger was severely beaten and hospitalized. Lorenzo was the only one of his group of friends caught.

Lorenzo served 18 months for assault in a youth detention center. When he got out I was just starting high school. By the end of junior high I had finally managed to control my temper and concentrate on academics. I had fewer and fewer outbursts each year, and was only suspended once in junior high. Wanting to keep my options open I promised myself I would take high school seriously and my grades improved. I didn't know where I would want to go to college, but with good grades I would be able to take my pick. I developed self-discipline and put a lot of pressure on myself to succeed.... After earning enough credits to graduate a year early, I decided to travel for the better part of my senior year. Lorenzo was back in school also. Before long he had finished high school and was working on his associate degree at Monroe College in New York.

When Lorenzo was only a few credits away from finishing his degree, he was arrested again. This time it was for robbery. He had broken into a house and was sentenced to five years.

Throughout his story, Lorenzo emphasized his poor choices and blown opportunities. He also pointed out that he was more mature now and would be able to avoid being reincarcerated once he got out of prison. He insisted that despite all of the challenges I'd faced, the choices I had made were better and that I deserved full credit for my successes. He was right that people make choices.

Poor Odds

Needless to say Lorenzo and I did not choose the color of our skins. Lorenzo is black and I am white and we live in a country that incarcerates African-American men at a rate of 6,926/100,000, and white men at a rate of 919/100,000. Lorenzo is 23 years old. Thirty-two percent of black men in their twenties are under some type of correctional control—prison, parole, or probation, while only 6.6 percent white men are under correctional control. In New York State, African Americans make up 12.4 percent of the population but 50.4 percent of those behind bars. In fact non-Hispanic Caucasians make up a paltry 15.5 percent of the prison population. Perhaps our choices paved our individual ways, but I felt that the odds had been stacked from the beginning.

Consider drug offenses as an example. African-Americans constitute 13 percent of the population and a proportionate percentage of all monthly drug users, yet represent 35 percent of arrests for drug possession, 55 percent of convictions and 74 percent of prison sentences for drug related crimes. Just like Lorenzo's mother, 92 percent of female drug offenders serving time in NY State are women of color while it is estimated that whites account for at least 50 percent of drug use and drug offenses. Lorenzo's skin color makes him a member of the majority in prisons, but his education makes him a minority. He is close to earning his associate degree, while an estimated 65 percent of male inmates have neither a high school diploma nor a GED [general educational development, or general equivalency degree].

A partial explanation for these trends is that criminals tend to come from economically disadvantaged families, and a disproportionate number of economically disadvantaged families are minority. But this explanation does not justify an incarceration rate for black men of more than seven and a half times that of white men. Simply by being born a black male in the USA, Lorenzo faced a 29 percent chance of being incarcerated at some point in his life. Further, the chance of incarceration for black men in Brooklyn are considerably higher.

As a white man, I have a 4 percent chance of being incarcerated. My neighborhood, Hyde Park, and prep school, decrease that chance even further. If Lorenzo's skin did not affect his decision-making capabilities, then the numbers must have had some significance. Lorenzo's actions resulted in his incarceration, but I still feel that the color of my skin helped keep me out of jail. Lorenzo knows the realities of our criminal justice system far better than I do. He accepted my statistics but still refused to discount his own poor decisions.

Burden Faced by the Children

The Thursday morning we met was Lorenzo's first day off work in four months. He works serving breakfast and lunch from four in the morning until one in the afternoon, seven days a week. His job in the mess hall of one of the toughest prisons in New York State pays $0.26 an hour. He has been on "good behavior" and with his parole date only two years off, his counselor recently offered him a transfer to a medium security prison. Lorenzo decided not to accept the offer. Explaining this decision to me, he said "it would be easier to use the move to break up [his] two years." He was in a good routine, working seven days a week. He would wait another year before transferring to the less repressive and disciplined medium security prison. He was going to make sure he was ready this time.

Our visit ended and I caught a bus back to New Haven. Lorenzo has since written me that our visit inspired him to read widely and think about his upcoming parole date. Our debate reminded me of the burden faced by children of incarcerated parents. Concern over crime has been mounting, as have the number of prisoners in this country.

What about their children? We outnumber the total number of convicts in the US, yet are not guilty of any crime. Is it time for our government to take a more holistic, long-term approach to reducing crime, one that considers the effect of parental incarceration? The war on crime, and drugs in particular, has effectively created a generation of parentless children. Many of us will become incarcerated at some point ourselves. Before our visit it was easy for me to say, using statistics as evidence, that Lorenzo never had a chance. But meeting with him was an intense reminder that statistics are simply numbers. Prisoners are dynamic human beings. For the time being Lorenzo is in prison, but he will always be more than just a convict. Despite the statistics, people make choices that alter the courses of our lives; that does not mean that we all have the same choices available to us.

Lorenzo and I suffered tragedies as children, but compared to some, even other children with incarcerated parents, we were both privileged in many ways. The contradiction that still troubles me is the different perspectives Lorenzo and I chose. I could argue that my successes so far, overcoming overwhelming odds and difficulties along the way, are purely a result of my choices, hard work, and self-discipline. Instead, I know my successes were made possible by those very difficulties.

Instead of taking credit for where I am, I choose to point fingers. Instead of pointing fingers, Lorenzo chooses to take responsibility. Of course, we are both right, and both wrong. It is impossible to know where Lorenzo and I would be today if our parents had never been arrested, and we both made decisions within the context of our lives. The biggest problem is that too few children with incarcerated parents have adequate options available—too few live in environments that encourage success.

Once on the street, Lorenzo hopes to finish his degree and perhaps become a counselor. I have not thought much beyond Yale. I have not yet decided on my career path, but next year I will choose a major and perhaps eventually attend a graduate school. In the meantime, I hope to maintain my friendship with Lorenzo and eagerly anticipate meeting him outside of the confines of a prison visiting room for the first time in our lives.

Organizations to Contact

Aid to Children of Imprisoned Mothers Inc.
906 Ralph David Abernathy Blvd. SW, Atlanta, GA   30310
(404) 755-3262 • fax: (404) 755-3294
e-mail: barnhill@takingaim.net
Web site: www.takingaim.net/

Aid to Children of Imprisoned Mothers is a nonprofit, community-based organization that assists inmate mothers, their children, and other family members in maintaining critically important family ties during the mother's incarceration. It publishes a newsletter, the *Mentor*, twice a year.

American Correctional Association (ACA)
4380 Forbes Blvd., Lanham, MD   20706-4322
(301) 918-1800 • fax: (301) 918-1900
e-mail: www.aca.org
Web site: www.aca.org/

The ACA is committed to improving national and international correctional policy and to promoting the professional development of those working in the field of corrections. It offers a variety of books and correspondence courses on corrections and criminal justice and publishes the bimonthly magazine *Corrections Today*.

Cato Institute
1000 Massachusetts Ave. NW, Washington, DC   20001-5403
(202) 842-0200 • fax: (202) 842-3490
e-mail: cato@cato.org
Web site: www.cato.org

The Cato Institute is a libertarian public policy research foundation dedicated to limiting the role of government and protecting individual liberties. The institute evaluates government policies and offers reform proposals in its publication *Policy Analysis*. Topics include "Prison Blues: How America's Foolish Sentencing Policies Endanger Public Safety" and "Crime, Police, and Root Causes." In addition, the institute publishes the quarterly magazine *Regulation*, the bimonthly *Cato Policy Report*, and numerous books.

Center for Alternative Sentencing and Employment Services (CASES)
346 Broadway, 8th Fl., New York, NY   10013
(212) 732-0076 • fax: (212) 571-0292
e-mail: info@cases.org
Web site: www.cases.org/

CASES seeks to end what it views as the overuse of incarceration as a response to crime. It operates two alternative-sentencing programs in New York City: (1) the Court Employment Project, which provides intensive supervision and services for felony offenders, and (2) the Community Service Sentencing Project, which works with repeat misdemeanor offenders. The center advocates in court for such offenders' admission into its programs. It publishes various program brochures.

Center for Children with Incarcerated Parents (CCIP)
PO Box 41-286, Eagle Rock, CA   90041
(626) 449-2470
e-mail: ccip@earthlink.net
Web site: www.e-ccip.org

Founded in 1989 by Denise Johnston and Katherine Gabel, the mission of CCIP is the prevention of crime and incarceration. The center services agencies working with families involved in the criminal justice system. CCIP provides parent mentoring, family support services, child and caregiver support groups, referrals and placements for families that are failing to supervise their children, and entrepreneurial training for children of prisoners.

Families Against Mandatory Minimums (FAMM)

1612 K St. NW, Suite 1400, Washington, DC   20006

(202) 822-6700 • fax: (202) 822-6704

e-mail: famm@famm.org

Web site: www.famm.org

FAMM works to end unjust mandatory minimum sentencing laws, change U.S. policy toward drug laws, and prepare clemency petitions for federal prisoners. It publishes a free newsletter.

Family and Corrections Network

32 Oak Grove Rd., Palmyra, VA   22963

(434) 589-3036 • fax: (434) 589-6520

e-mail: fcn@fcnetwork.org

Web site: www.fcnetwork.org/

The members of the Family and Corrections Network offer information, training, and technical assistance for children of prisoners. The organization also conducts parenting programs for prisoners and sponsors hospitality programs to help incarcerated fathers and mothers keep in touch with their children.

Federal Bureau of Prisons

320 First St. NW, Washington, DC   20534

e-mail: webmaster@bop.gov

Web site: www.bop.gov

The Federal Bureau of Prisons is part of the U.S. Department of Justice. The bureau works to protect society by confining offenders in the controlled environments of prisons and community-based facilities. It believes in providing work and other self-improvement opportunities within these facilities to assist offenders in becoming law-abiding citizens. The bureau publishes the annual *State of the Bureau* as well as other information.

The Heritage Foundation
214 Massachusetts Ave. NE, Washington, DC   20002
(202) 546-4400 • fax: (202) 546-8328
e-mail: pubs@heritage.org
Web site: www.heritage.org

The Heritage Foundation is a conservative public policy research institute. A proponent of limited government, it advocates tougher sentencing and the construction of more prisons. The foundation publishes articles on a variety of public policy issues in its *Backgrounder* series and also offers many books by foundation scholars on its Web site.

John Howard Society
809 Blackburn Mews, Kingston, ON   K7P 2N6
  Canada
(613) 384-6272 • fax: (613) 384-1847
e-mail: national@johnhoward.ca
Web site: www.johnhoward.ca

The John Howard Society of Canada advocates reform in the criminal justice system and monitors governmental policy to ensure fair and compassionate treatment of prisoners. It views imprisonment as a last resort. The organization provides education for the community, support services for at-risk youth, and rehabilitation programs for former inmates. Its publications include the booklet *Literacy and the Courts: Protecting the Right to Understand.*

Justice Fellowship
PO Box 16069, Washington, DC   20041-6069
(703) 456-4050 • fax (703) 478-9679
e-mail: mail@justicefellowship.org
Web site: www.justicefellowship.org

Justice Fellowship is a nonprofit public policy organization dedicated to advancing biblically based restorative justice principles throughout the United States. It advocates restitution and reconciliation and the right of victims to play a meaning-ful role in the criminal justice process. Its publications include the book *Restoring Justice* and the bimonthly *Justice Report.*

National Center on Institutions and Alternatives (NCIA)
7222 Ambassador Rd., Baltimore, MD   21244
(410) 265-1490 • fax: (410) 597-9656
e-mail: HHoelter@nciamd.org
Web site: www.ncianet.org/ncia

NCIA is a criminal justice foundation that encourages community-based alternatives to prison that are more effec-tive in providing the education, training, and personal skills required for the rehabilitation of nonviolent offenders. The center advocates doubling "good conduct" credit for the early release of nonviolent first-time offenders in the federal system to make room for violent offenders. NCIA publishes books, reports, and the periodic newsletters *Criminal Defense Update* and *Jail Suicide/Mental Health Update.*

National Prison Project
American Civil Liberties Union, Washington, DC   20009
(202) 234-4830 • fax: (202) 234-4890
e-mail: aclu@aclu.org
Web site: www.aclu.org/prison

Formed in 1972, the National Prison Project serves as a na-tional resource center and litigates cases to strengthen and protect adult and juvenile offenders' Eighth Amendment rights. It opposes electronic monitoring of offenders and the privatization of prisons. The project publishes the quarterly *National Prison Project Journal* and various booklets.

PEN, Writing Program for Prisoners
568 Broadway, New York, NY   10012
(212) 334-1660
e-mail: pen@pen.org
Web site: www.pen.org/

Founded in 1971, PEN's Writing Program for Prisoners sponsors an annual writing contest, publishes a free handbook for prisoners, provides one-on-one mentoring to inmates whose writing shows merit or promise, conducts workshops for former inmates, and seeks to get inmates' work to the public through literary publications and readings.

Police Foundation
1201 Connecticut Ave. NW, Washington, DC   20036
(202) 833-1460 • fax: (202) 659-9149
e-mail: pfinfo@policefoundation.org
Web site: www.policefoundation.org

The Police Foundation is committed to increasing the effectiveness of police in controlling crime, maintaining order, and providing humane and efficient service. The foundation sponsors forums that debate and disseminate ideas to improve personnel and practice in American criminal policing. It publishes a number of books, reports, and handbooks regarding all aspects of the criminal justice system.

Prison Activist Resource Center (PARC)
1920 Park Ave., Berkeley, CA   94701
(510) 893-4648 • fax: (510) 893-4607
e-mail: webmaster@prisonactivist.org
Web site www.prisonactivist.org/parc/

PARC is an all-volunteer organization that provides support for educators, activists, prisoners, and prisoners' families. PARC's mission is to educate the public about the need for prison abolition and to offer support and resources for anti-prison activists.

Prison Fellowship Ministries
PO Box 17500, Washington, DC   20041-0500
(703) 478-0100
Web site: www.prisonfellowship.org

Prison Fellowship Ministries encourages Christians to work in prisons and to assist communities in ministering to prisoners, ex-offenders, and their families. It works toward establishing a fair, effective criminal justice system and trains volunteers for in-prison ministries. Publications include the monthly *Jubilee* newsletter, the quarterly *Justice Report*, and numerous books, including *Born Again* and *Life Sentence*.

The Sentencing Project

514 Tenth St. NW, Suite 1000, Washington, DC   20004
(202) 628-0871 • fax: (202) 628-1091
e-mail: staff@sentencingproject.org
Web site: www.sentencingproject.org

The Sentencing Project seeks to provide public defenders and other public officials with information on establishing and improving alternative sentencing programs that provide convicted persons with positive, constructive options to incarceration. It promotes increased public understanding of the sentencing process and alternative sentencing programs. It publishes many fact sheets, papers, and reports, including *Americans Behind Bars: A Comparison of International Rates of Incarceration* and *Young Black Men and the Criminal Justice System: A Growing National Problem.*

United States Sentencing Commission

One Columbus Circle NE, Washington, DC   20002-8002
(202) 502-4500
e-mail: pubaffairs@ussc.gov
Web site: www.ussc.gov

The United States Sentencing Commission is an independent federal agency that collects data about crime and sentencing and helps develop guidelines for sentencing in federal courts. The commission also trains criminal justice professionals in the use of the guidelines and serves as a clearinghouse of crime and sentencing information for the federal government, criminal justice professionals, and the public. The commission publishes annual reports, occasional newsletters, and reports to Congress, including *Special Report to the Congress: Cocaine and Federal Sentencing Policy.*

For Further Research

Books

Lloyd C. Anderson, *Voices from a Southern Prison.* Athens: University of Georgia Press, 2000.

Allison Campbell, Andrew Coyle, and Rodney Neufeld, eds., *Capitalist Punishment: Prison Privatization and Human Rights.* Atlanta: Clarity, 2003.

Holley Cantine, ed., *Prison Etiquette: The Convict's Compendium of Useful Information.* Carbondale: Southern Illinois University Press, 2001.

Angela Y. Davis, *Are Prisons Obsolete?* New York: Seven Stories, 2003.

Victoria R. DeRosia, *Living Inside Prison Walls: Adjustment Behavior.* Westport, CT: Praeger, 1998.

Mark Dow, *American Gulag: Inside U.S. Immigration Prisons.* Berkeley and Los Angeles: University of California Press, 2004.

Joseph T. Hallinan, *Going Up the River: Travels in a Prison Nation.* New York: Random House, 2001.

Tara Herivel and Paul Wright, *Prison Nation: The Warehousing of America's Poor.* New York: Routledge, 2003.

Paula C. Johnson, *Inner Lives: Voices of African American Women in Prison.* New York: New York University Press, 2003.

Lorna A. Rhodes, *Total Confinement: Madness and Reason in the Maximum Security Prison.* Berkeley and Los Angeles: University of California Press, 2004.

David J. Rothman, ed., *The Oxford History of the Prison: The Practice of Punishment in Western Society.* New York: Oxford University Press, 1995.

Stephen Stanko, Wayne Gillespie, and Gordon A. Crews, *Living in Prison: A History of the Correctional System with an Insider's View*. Westport, CT: Greenwood 2004.

David S. Tanenhaus, *Juvenile Justice in the Making*. New York: Oxford University Press, 2004.

Hans Toch, *Mosaic of Despair: Human Breakdowns in Prison*. Washington, DC: American Psychological Association, 1992.

Michael Tonry, *Thinking About Crime: Sense and Sensibility in American Penal Culture*. New York: Oxford University Press, 2004.

Michael Tonry, ed., *The Future of Imprisonment*. New York: Oxford University Press, 2004.

James Q. Whitman, ed., *Harsh Justice: Criminal Punishment and the Widening Divide between America and Europe*. New York: Oxford University Press, 2003.

Richard Wortley, *Situational Prison Control: Crime Prevention in Correctional Institutions*. Cambridge: Cambridge University Press, 2002.

Jennifer Wynn, *Inside Rikers: Stories from the World's Largest Penal Colony*. New York: St. Martin's, 2001.

Periodicals

Sasha Abramsky, "Incarceration, Inc.: Private Prisons Thrive on Cheap Labor and the Hunger of Job-Starved Towns," *Nation*, July 19, 2004.

Noel Brinkerhoff, "Lock 'Em Up?" *California Journal*, February 1999.

Nina Chernoff and Robert Johnson, "'Opening a Vein': Inmate Poetry and the Prison Experience," *Prison Journal*, June 2002.

Alison Chin, "Increasing the Accountability of State Actors in Prison Systems: A Necessary Enterprise in Guaranteeing the Eighth Amendment Rights of Prison Inmates," *Journal of Criminal Law and Criminology*, Winter 2003.

Nora V. Demleitner, "Smart Public Policy: Replacing Imprisonment with Targeted Nonprison Sentences and Collateral Sanctions," *Stanford Law Review*, October 2005.

Margaret Gabriel, "A Journey Behind Prison Walls: Delegation of Kentucky Catholics Brings Community to Penitentiary," *National Catholic Reporter*, September 19, 2003.

Thomas F. Geraghty, "Prisons and After Prison," *Journal of Criminal Law and Criminology*, Summer 2004.

Alfred Himelson, "Prison Programs That Produce," *World and I*, December 2003.

John Kampfner, "Our Incarceration Rate Is 'Scary,'" *New Statesman*, May 31, 2004.

Nathan Koppel, "Less Cruel, More Usual: Alvin Bronstein's Career Move as Prisoner Advocate," *American Lawyer*, May 2004.

Drew Leder, "Imprisoned Bodies: The Life-World of the Incarcerated," *Social Justice*, Spring/Summer 2004.

Daniel L. Lombardo and Robert N. Levy, "To Confine or Not to Confine: Community-Based Corrections," *Corrections Today*, December 2002.

Ayelish McGarvey, "Reform Done Right: A Chicago Program Demonstrates the Logic of Preparing Prisoners for Life on the Outside," *American Prospect*, December 2003.

Joycelyn M. Pollock, "Parenting Programs in Women's Prison," *Women & Criminal Justice*, Winter 2003.

Dorothy E. Roberts, "The Social and Moral Cost of Mass Incarceration in African American Communities," *Stanford Law Review*, April 2004.

Paul J. Silvia, "Throwing Away the Key: Measuring Prison Reform Attitudes," *Journal of Applied Social Psychology*, December 2003.

Jens Soering, "He Who Has Eyes," *America*, August 18, 2003.

Vivien Stern, "Looking Beyond the Borders: Improving Correctional Standards Worldwide," *Corrections Today*, February 2002.

Margaret Talbot, "Catch and Release," *Atlantic Monthly*, January/February 2003.

Index